TABOR EVANS

LONGARM

AND THE COLORADO GUNDOWN

JOVE BOOKS, NEW YORK

LONGARM AND THE COLORADO GUNDOWN

A Jove Book / published by arrangement with
the author

PRINTING HISTORY
Jove edition / October 1991

ISBN: 0-515-10689-5

Jove Books are published by The Berkley Publishing Group,
200 Madison Avenue, New York, New York 10016.
The name "JOVE" and the "J" logo
are trademarks belonging to Jove Publications, Inc.

JUSTICE AT GUNPOINT

"We'll be in Tipson in ten minutes or less," Bevvy called to the men in the coach. "Everybody get ready."

There was a rattle of steel clashing on steel when Winchester levers were cranked as the posse members checked the function of their guns. Others snapped shotgun breeches open to inspect their chambers and make sure the guns were charged with man-sized buckshot and not puny bird shot. If there was any shooting tonight it would be to kill, not to scare . . .

LONGARM

AND THE COLORADO GUNDOWN

Chapter 1

Longarm clamped his lips shut to contain the belch that was surging out of his stomach. He was able to keep from embarrassing himself, but he wasn't able to stop himself from burping. The liver flavor was just fine this second time around, but the onions tasted a trifle stale.

He was just back from lunch, and normally would've let it rip if he needed to belch in the U.S. Marshal's office. In fact, he might've tried to amplify things just to see if he could get a rise out of Marshal Vail's dignified—a polite way of saying stuffy—clerk Henry.

Not this time, though.

There was a young lady standing bent over Henry's desk signing something there. Longarm sure as hell didn't want to disturb her. In fact, if she wanted to spend the rest of the afternoon bent over like that, well, Longarm would be so damned polite that he'd just stand right where he was and not interrupt for nothing.

The view from back there was what you might call fine. Just fine.

Unfortunately, the lady's business seemed to be completed once her signature was done. She returned the steel-nibbed pen to Henry and straightened, diminishing the quality of the view somewhat once her gown was no longer stretched tight across the rear portions of her anatomy.

"That should be everything, Miss Mayweather," Henry said. "Thank you for bringing this to our attention."

"Thank *you,* sir." Mmm, not a bad voice, Longarm decided. Sexy.

She turned, and he decided he didn't regret losing that back view after all. This was one handsome filly. Blonde, perky, apple cheeks, ample chest—more than ample, in fact damned well overflowing. Yes, indeedy, the view from the front was fine too.

He smiled and gave her a small bow. "Ma'am."

"Hello." She had dimples when she smiled. Longarm liked dimples. "Are you the marshal, sir?"

"A deputy, ma'am." He bowed and held his brown Stetson low. "United States Deputy Marshal Custis Long, ma'am. At your service."

He was glad now that he'd stopped at the barber's on his way to lunch today, and that his hat and jacket were as freshly brushed and decent-looking as either was likely to get. He looked, in fact, pretty much his best at the moment.

Not that Longarm found anything about himself to get het up about. But the ladies didn't real often object to what they saw when he was around.

He was above six feet in height, with broad shoulders and a horseman's narrow-waisted, muscular-legged build. He had brown hair and a large sweep of dark brown mustache set on a tanned and weathered face. He wore brown corduroy trousers and a brown tweed coat, and a flannel shirt under a brown calfskin vest. His stovepipe cavalry boots were black, as was the gunbelt that circled his waist. The butt of a .44-caliber Colt Lightning showed in a cross-draw holster at the front of the coat. A gold watch chain crossed the front of his vest, although only one end of the chain was put to a normal use. The fob end was soldered to the butt of a .44-caliber double-barreled derringer. Not that he was thinking in terms of weaponry at the moment.

"Perhaps you shall be assigned to work on my case, Mr. Long," the lady suggested.

"It'd be a pleasure as well as a duty, ma'am."

2

She beamed. "Wonderful." She turned to Henry and said, "Make a note of that, would you please? Mr. Long is to be my deputy."

"I'll, uh, do that, Miss Mayweather," Henry said. For some reason Henry looked kinda like he was having a gas pain. He coughed and turned away, took his spectacles off, and began polishing the lenses with a handkerchief.

"Thank you. Yes. Thank you very much." She turned back to Longarm. "Shall we begin, Mr. Long?"

Longarm was going to say something, but damned Henry went and interrupted. "Miss Mayweather."

"Yes?"

"Deputy Long can't start work on your case, you understand, until the marshal himself makes the assignment. What you should do, miss, is go home now and wait for the assigned deputy to contact you."

"Really? But I've already told you to write down there that it is Mr. Long that I want. I distinctly specified that, did I not?"

"You did, miss, and I've made a note of it, so I have. I will see that your wishes are conveyed to Marshal Vail. But you do understand that Deputy Long cannot begin work on your, um, case until Marshal Vail releases him from his other duties. You do understand that, don't you?"

"Of course I understand that, but . . ."

"Please. Trust us, Miss Mayweather. I assure you that Marshal Vail will be informed at the earliest possible opportunity. Just as soon as he returns from Omaha."

Miss Mayweather made a pouting face toward Henry, then flashed a radiant smile at Longarm. "I look forward to seeing you again, Mr. Long." She curtsied.

Longarm returned the gesture with another bow, a rather more shallow one this time, and held the door so the pretty lady could make her exit into the hallways of the Federal Building on the fringes of Denver's downtown district.

Then he turned back to Henry with a frown. "Omaha? When the . . ." He turned back and opened the door a crack so he could glance out and make sure Miss Mayweather

3

wasn't within hearing any longer. "What the hell is this about Billy going t' Omaha? He was right here just a little while ago."

Henry chuckled. The slight clerk hooked the earpieces of his glasses behind one ear and then the other, and returned his handkerchief to a pocket. "You know as well as I do that Billy is in his office, Longarm."

"Then what . . . ?"

Henry winked and handed Longarm the form Miss Mayweather had just signed.

Confused, Longarm took the thing and skimmed over it.

Then he laughed. "Shit. You're kidding."

"May be," Henry said with a grin. "But Miss Mayweather isn't."

"Shit," Longarm repeated. He looked down and read the official complaint again. "Shee-double-it," he said this time when he was done.

Henry laughed.

According to the report, filled out in the lady's own hand and duly signed with Henry as a witness, she was asking the United States Marshal, First District Court of Colorado, to intercept, apprehend, and prosecute a host of demons who were invading her privacy every night. The demons entered her head, she said, by way of her nose. And they were awfully annoying. She, uh, wanted them arrested.

"Sounds like a job for the sheriff t' me," Longarm suggested.

"Oh, she's tried there already. Also the city police. *They* sent her here."

"We'll have t' do something nice for them someday. Anybody figure out how we have federal jurisdiction over this?"

"I asked her about that," Henry admitted. "She thinks the demons might get their orders through the mail. That sounds to me like something Jim Sanders over at the police department might have dreamed up and suggested to her, just to get her off his back and onto ours."

4

"Obviously a federal case then," Longarm agreed dryly. "You still want to ask Billy to assign you to it?"

"Mmm, reckon I'd normally want t' snap this one up. I mean, hell, think of all the glory. It ain't everybody gets to arrest a whole gang of demons. But now that I think on it, I'm pretty busy. Give this'un to Smiley. You know he's always game for a good laugh." Smiley was perhaps the most taciturn and gloomy human being Custis Long had ever met. Smiley would shit little green apples if he was ever handed a "case" like this one.

Henry chuckled again, wadded the official report into a crumpled ball, and deposited it into the file it was best suited for—the one beside his desk whose contents were hauled away and burned each night.

"Seriously, Longarm, if you are quite ready to get back to work now, the marshal wants to see you."

"I dunno, Henry. I may be missin' out on the case of my life by not goin' after Miss Mayweather. But I expect I'll risk it." He laughed and went to tap on Billy Vail's office door.

Chapter 2

Billy Vail looked up when Longarm came in, grunted once, and gave the paperwork on his desk a frown of concentration as he bent back to it. "Be with you in a second," he said.

Longarm helped himself to a seat in front of his boss's desk and pulled out a slim, evil-looking cheroot. He took his time about trimming the twist off the tip, moistening the wrapper leaf on his tongue, and lighting the smoke. Wasn't no way, he reflected, that he would ever want to swap jobs with Billy. A United States marshal had to be an administrator, a paper-pusher, much more than he was allowed to be a lawman. Custis Long knew he made a fair hand as a lawman, but lacked the patience to be any kind of administrator. In particular he lacked the thick skin that was required when a man had to deal with politicians. Billy Vail didn't like that part of the job a lick more than his top deputy would have. The difference was that Billy was able to put up with it. Longarm was convinced he never could.

Billy finished the form he was scratching on, put it atop a pile of other papers, dipped his pen nib into the inkwell, and scrawled something onto another sheet and then another. Finally he let out a sigh before bellowing for Henry, who came in and took that stack of papers away. There were plenty more remaining on the desk still to be attended to.

"Deputy Long," Billy said by way of greeting.

Longarm crossed his legs and grinned at him. "Marshal Vail."

"You don't have to look so smug, damn you," Billy said accusingly.

Longarm's grin didn't waver. "I think you need a drink, Boss."

Billy kneaded his face with the palms of both hands and sighed again. The impromptu massage made his already pink complexion even redder. He ran one hand back over his scalp, a gesture of habit, not necessity. There no longer was hair growing there to be smoothed down.

"What I need," Billy said, "is a thirty-hour day. Twenty-four just isn't enough anymore." He grimaced, then shrugged as if to say what the hell, he hadn't taken the job in search of a vacation anyway. "What can I do for you, Longarm?"

"Oh, a raise would be nice, I suppose." Longarm held the cheroot between his teeth and grinned.

"Is that what you came to see me about, dammit? If that's all it is, well, I have work to do. More important things than to—"

"Billy. Whoa. *You* sent for *me*. Remember?"

"I did?" The marshal seemed taken aback by that. He sat up in his creaking swivel chair and blinked once. Then comprehension dawned and he made a rueful face. That lasted only an instant before he smiled. "Could be you're right. Could be I do need a drink. Or something." He reached into a stack of paperwork and rooted through the sheets and folders until he found the one he wanted. "There's a writ of habeas corpus here that needs serving, Longarm."

"Service of a writ, Billy? Damn, can't you find something more interesting for me to do than that?" Longarm detested simple, boring, routine matters like this. He much preferred to be out digging and scraping and tending to real criminals than playing hey-boy for the courts and the fancy-pants judges.

"As a matter of fact, Longarm, I probably could. But in this particular matter, you were asked for by name."

"Why me?"

7

"Now that's an age-old complaint, isn't it," Billy mused. "The eternal question, Custis. Why me? I ask it myself sometimes. Of course, it isn't all that often any of us gets an answer to it." The marshal smiled. "This time you happen to be in luck. I actually know the answer to it."

Billy was obviously in something of a mood today. Longarm went over to the cabinet where the marshal kept a little something for the oiling of troubled waters. He poured a brandy for Billy and a rye whiskey for himself while the marshal nattered on.

"You remember a case a while back where you were in close, um, contact with the Ute Indian tribe?"

"Not quite th' whole tribe," Longarm answered. When it came to close, well, there was one Ute in particular he'd gotten close to. Pretty little thing she'd been too.

"You know what I mean."

"I might could," Longarm agreed.

"For some reason the Utes liked you. And apparently trust you. That's why you are being asked to serve this writ."

"I see," Longarm said. "More or less. Is begging gonna get me outta this?"

"Nope, no chance."

"Then I expect you better tell me 'bout it."

"All right. The Utes asked for you, like I said. That request was passed along through their attorney."

Longarm's eyebrows shot up. An attorney representing the Ute nation? Now wasn't that a strange kettle o' fish. Generally these cases involved some bunch of greedy whites filing papers to hustle Indians out of their way, not the Indians filing papers themselves.

"Was there something you wanted, Longarm?"

"No, you go ahead, Billy. I'll cough an' marvel when you're done."

"Thank you. As I was saying, the Utes requested your participation in particular. That was passed along by the attorney representing their interests. A brief was filed with

8

Judge John McFee, and he . . . Longarm, you look like you're ready to bust. Is there something you want to ask me?"

"It's just . . . who the hell is this McFee? I sure thought I knew every judge in this district. And I never heard of no McFee."

"McFee is federal. He sits in Nebraska."

"There ain't no Utes in Nebraska, Billy. Not unless I've got awful forgetful all o' a sudden."

"There may not be Ute Indians there, Longarm, but there are federal courts in Nebraska. Including Judge McFee's. I might point out that there is also precedent there. Newly made case law that originated in Omaha. And that is what we are dealing with here. Are you familiar with Standing Bear versus Crook?"

"Mmm, I can't say as that turned up on my reading list yet. But I'm sure I'll get to it real soon."

"The case was in Judge Elmer Dundy's court recently. Judge Dundy came up with a habeas corpus ruling that says Indians are entitled to the same privileges and protections as anyone else—the same obligations of compliance with the law too, of course—if they choose to live off their assigned reservation lands."

"Now ain't that an unusual notion," Longarm said dryly.

"Perhaps. The point is, Dundy's ruling means that Indians who are causing no harm have the right to leave their reservations if they wish and conduct themselves as any citizen might."

"Causing no harm," Longarm repeated. He took a drag on his cheroot and stared toward the ceiling while he slowly expelled the smoke. "An' who is it, Billy, who decides if these here Indians are causing harm or not?"

Vail gave him a tight-lipped smile. "That is what cuts to the heart of it, Longarm. As long as any Indian anywhere in this country wants to go to war with us whites, most whites are going to assume that any Indian off any reservation is out for scalps and glory. The interpretation of intent is where things get complicated."

9

"Sounds t' me like there's a disagreement over the intention o' some Utes," Longarm guessed.

"In a nutshell, yes. A small group of Utes have been detained by lawful authority in a town called Snowshoe. I gather there is one faction in town that wants those and any other Utes in that part of the country rounded up and shipped back onto their reservation lands. Others, I understand, think the problem would be best served by hanging the ones in custody and shooting all the ones who aren't."

Longarm grunted.

"We come into it because some lawyer named Ab Able is sharper than you are when it comes to case law. Able filed a request for the habeas corpus writ before Judge McFee, citing the Dundy precedent in support of the petition. The writ was granted. And you've been asked to serve it."

"Filed it in Nebraska, not here."

"For obvious reasons," Billy said.

Longarm nodded. He understood those reasons quite as well as Marshal Vail did. Snowshoe was a mining camp in the San Juan Mountains of southwestern Colorado, not terribly far from the Ute reservation. Logically any relevant petitions would have been filed with a federal court in Denver, closest to the scene, so to speak. But it hadn't been very long ago when the Ute nation had rebelled against their agent. There had been a massacre of whites at the agency headquarters at the time. Other whites unlucky enough to be there on the wrong day had been beaten, and several women raped but not killed. Before it was all over troops had had to be rushed in, and a pitched battle had been fought. The army had won the fight, but there'd been casualties on both sides of the conflict. Feelings still ran high about that in Colorado, and trigger fingers were still somewhat shaky. Any judge in Colorado would've known about that. And if the guy was worried about his own political future, he might've been plenty reluctant to follow Judge Dundy's example from Nebraska and allow a habeas corpus release for the Utes regardless of guilt or innocence.

"Lawyer Able ain't stupid," Longarm observed.

"No, he isn't."

"So now I go down t' Snowshoe and spring these Utes outta the local calaboose, is that it?"

"That would seem to be it, yes."

Longarm grinned. "Lawyer Able might be smart. But he sure ain't shy about making me the most unpopular son of a bitch in Snowshoe, Colorado, is he?"

"If it makes you feel any better, Longarm, you can cling to this thought. It's only the whites who might want to shoot you in the back. The Utes will still think you're a swell fellow."

"Yeah, that does make me feel a whole heap better, Billy. Thanks for the encouragement." He grinned and tossed off the rye that he hadn't gotten around to tasting yet.

"Giving aid and comfort to my deputies is what I'm here for, Longarm," Billy said dryly.

"We always figured there had t' be some reason. Nice t' know what it is at long last."

"Henry can arrange for your expense vouchers, Longarm. Do I need to mention that the quicker you handle this one the better it will be for everyone?"

"Believe me, Billy, the quicker I can get in there and hurry the hell back out the happier I'll be too. I don't wanta set myself up as a target any longer'n I have to."

"And do watch your backside, Longarm. The paperwork is just murder when a federal employee dies on the job. I haven't got time for it."

"Your concern is touching, Boss."

Billy winked at him and bent over the thick, messy piles of papers on his desk again. Longarm got up and retrieved the signed writ Billy had pushed over to the edge of the desk. He headed for the doorway. He was halfway through it when Billy coughed and in a soft, serious voice said, "Take care, Custis." Longarm paused, nodded, and pulled the door closed behind him.

Chapter 3

There was, in truth, no really good way to get from Denver to Snowshoe. At least none that Custis Long knew of. And while he had never been to that exact mining camp, he had certainly been to others just like it in the same neighborhood. There just wasn't any direct rail connection, not yet, although the railroads were building as hard and fast as track could be laid from one place to another.

Longarm went into a huddle with Henry about the various possibilities, then collected a fistful of expense vouchers.

"Better take some travel vouchers too," Henry advised. "Some of those new little rail and coach lines won't accept a badge as a pass."

"The lines that don't have mail contracts, I take it?"

Henry grinned. "Don't have and probably won't have."

"I'll take some travel slips too then, if you please."

"I can have everything ready for you in forty-five minutes, Longarm."

"While you're doing that, I'll go lay in a supply of smokes. Man never knows what he'll run into in those mining camps. Might be champagne and oysters hauled in fresh in barrels of ice one place, or the cheapest alcohol and tobacco-juice rotgut in the next."

"And if I know you, Longarm, you'd rather the rotgut than the champagne."

Long gave Billy Vail's clerk a look of wounded innocence. "Please."

12

"Sorry. Now go on and buy your emergency supplies. I have work to do to get you ready."

"I'll be back in a half hour."

"Fine, but if you pester me I'll give your home address to Miss Mayweather."

"You wouldn't."

"Calling my bluff are you, Longarm?"

"I'll see you in an hour, Henry. Not a minute sooner."

Henry chuckled as Longarm scuttled out into the hallway on the double-quick.

The stagecoach jolted to a stop, the passengers rocking back and forth with the motion as the heavy wagon body bounced and twisted on the leather straps that were all it had in the way of springs.

"Whoa, dammit, whoa." The driver's voice reached in through the open window. A horse stamped a foot and there was the sound of bit chains rattling.

Longarm yawned and sat upright on the thinly upholstered coach seat.

"Are we there? Is this Telluride?" a querulous voice whined.

"Not yet," Longarm said patiently. "This oughta be Silver Creek."

The man who'd asked the question gave him a look like it was Longarm's fault the coach hadn't yet reached Telluride. Longarm was not going to be greatly disappointed to be parting company from this traveler. The salesman was going on to Telluride by coach, while Longarm would be transferring to a newly completed rail line here for the rest of the trip into Snowshoe. Thank goodness.

"Nice meetin' you," Longarm lied politely as he opened the coach door and dropped down to ground level without waiting for the wood steps to be set in place.

A boy dragged the steps up and put them beside the open door so the other passengers could disembark if they wished. There had been eleven men in the coach on this run. Not bad, everything considered. The Studebaker would accommodate an even dozen inside, plus there was room for more on the roof if necessary.

Longarm lighted a cheroot and waited patiently for the helper to get around to unloading luggage from the boot on the back of the coach and from the rack up top. Longarm's bag and saddle were in the roof rack and likely would be among the last things off. He really hadn't needed to be in any hurry to leave the coach. He yawned again and watched the men—pity there hadn't been any women traveling the route this trip—climb stiffly down to the ground. They'd all been cooped up inside the coach for the past four hours, ever since the last change of horses.

" . . . talked 'er down t' forty cents," one of the men was saying to his traveling companion, "but at that she got the best o' me 'cause she had the clap."

Longarm looked off down the street. Not that there was so very much to see in Silver Creek. The mining camp was raw and ugly, but busy with almost frantic activity as men rushed to claw as much treasure from the earth as they could before the next man beat them to it.

Mining claims only protected a man so far because if two outfits claimed different outcroppings of the same vein, the one who dug the quickest was the one who would be allowed to dig the most. Once they met somewhere underground they would both be out of business and looking for a fresh strike.

The half-finished stores, many of them still with canvas tenting material for roofs, were doing a booming trade, and freight rigs rumbled up and down the wide main street like a horde of gigantic scurrying ants.

About the only businesses that were not rushed at this time of day were the honky-tonks and the saloons. Those would not hit their stride until nightfall when the miners came off shift.

Longarm had never been to Silver Creek before. He hadn't needed to. Hell, he already knew the town well. This one and all the others just like it.

"Hey, you! This stuff belong t' you, mister?"

He turned. The stagecoach helper was holding Longarm's gear aloft.

"Yeah, that's mine."

"Take it now, mister, or buy it a ticket to Telluride, it don't make no difference t' me which."

"Then I expect I'll take it, thank you."

The boy tossed the bag first, then the saddle with Longarm's scabbarded Winchester attached.

The other coach passengers had already dispersed, the ones who were staying in Silver Creek straggling off in the direction of a hotel in the next block, the men unlucky enough to suffer more jostling throughout the night as the coach went on bolting for the nearest saloon.

Longarm decided against joining either party. What he needed was the terminus of the Silver Creek, Tipson, and Glory Narrow Gauge Rail Road. He had no idea when the next train would be scheduled out, but he intended to be on it. He flipped the butt of his cheroot into the street, shouldered his saddle, and picked up his bag.

Now all he needed was for someone to point the way.

Chapter 4

"Say *what*?" Longarm barked.

"Hey now, mister, it ain't my fault," the man snapped right back at him.

"But I was told—"

"Yeah, yeah, everybody was told. So now I'm telling you. The railroad ain't here. Yet, that is. Just a temporary little setback, see. It'll get built direc'ly. Just you wait an' see that it will."

"But dammit—"

"Mister, if there *was* a railroad here, d'you really think I'd lie about it? I mean, that's the sort of lie a fella could get caught out in real easy. You know? So take my word for it, friend. There ain't no railroad here just yet. But it'll be along." The fellow grinned, turned his head, and spat. "You're welcome t' wait for it if you want."

"Son of a *bitch*," Longarm complained.

But of course the man inside the offices of the Silver Creek, Tipson, and Glory Narrow Gauge Rail Road had heard all of that before. Maybe even several times. And it wasn't going to do anyone any good for Longarm to stand there and argue with him about passage on a railroad that did not yet exist.

"Sorry," Longarm said. "It's just—"

"Yeah, I know. Everybody's been told there's a line in. But it was only *scheduled* to be in by now. Wasn't never actually completed, see. The bosses kinda run outta money 'fore they got this far. They keep this office open for

16

when the rails do come through." He winked. "And for the investors. If you see what I mean."

"I'm afraid I do," Longarm said.

"If it helps you any, they did get part of the tracks laid. Tipson all the way t' Glory. An' a couple miles this side o' Glory too."

"What about Snowshoe?" Longarm asked.

"Pardon me?"

"I thought the road was supposed to connect with Snowshoe too."

The fellow laughed. "Lordy, mister, you have heard everything wrong, haven't you."

"Have I?"

"I'm afeered so. This line ain't supposed to go anywheres near Snowshoe. There's another narrow-gauge supposed to do that. The Bitterroot and Brightwater."

"The Bitterroot and Brightwater," Longarm repeated dully, not at all sure that this fellow wasn't pulling his leg now.

"That's right, mister. That line is the one supposed to run through Snowshoe. Our railroad never was intended t' get up there, not even when it's all the way done."

"But I thought—"

"Oh, I know. Easy enough mistake for a body t' make, our rights o' way bein' so close together. Why, I daresay on a map you could get mixed up which road was which. Except o' course they go different places. But for a piece there, they run right close together, the Bitterroot an' Brightwater being up high an' our grade down lower t' follow the streambeds, see. They figure to save miles by bridging, see, an' we figure t' save costs by wiggling around some. Does that make sense t' you, mister?"

"No," Longarm admitted.

"Well, don't let that bother you none. Fact is, their line ain't any closer to completion than ours is. But they got them some track laid same as we do. It's really Snowshoe you want to get to?"

"Yes, sir, it is."

"Then I expect I can help you, mister. We got a string o' wagons we run from Silver Creek t' our track-end. I can put you on a wagon if you're of a mind t' go. Carry you to the tracks, then on t' Glory. From there you can get a ride over top o' Twin Towers Mountain. That carries you over to the Bitterroot and Brightwater right of way, see, and you can get to Snowshoe easy from there."

The man was smiling.

Longarm felt like he was fixing to get a headache. And if he didn't, well, he was entitled to one anyhow.

"I would appreciate a ride on your wagon to Glory, friend."

"Kinda thought you might, neighbor. Be here a half hour past dawn tomorrow. 'Less you wanta wait another day, that is. Be all right if you want t' do that, see. Once you have your ticket you can hold onto it to use whenever you please."

The man was genial. Friendly. Pleasant. Cheerful. Helpful. Nice as nice could be.

Longarm felt an impulse to take the fellow by the throat and throttle him. "Dawn tomorrow will be fine," he said just as nicely as he knew how.

Chapter 5

Longarm had never been bound for Glory before. And the times he'd heard the expression used in the past, well, this wasn't exactly what he'd envisioned it would come to.

He suspected that at least part of his morning doubts came from last night's disappointments. There hadn't been a decent rye whiskey available anyplace in Silver Creek—though he'd sure as hell searched the saloons of the town just as diligently and sincerely as ever a man could hope to—and the bed he'd taken at one of the hotels had turned out to be lumpy. Also empty. Longarm had ended up going to bed half drunk and wholly horny, and his discontent from last night was carrying over into this morning's grumpiness.

He gave the mule-drawn wagon a baleful look. The rig was old and rickety and might give faithful service for the next twenty years. Or it might just as easily fall to pieces five miles down the road. The four mules that were hitched to it were small and scruffy, built more on the lines of house cats than draft stock, and made all the poorer to look at from the fact that their heavy coats from last winter hadn't yet fully shed off, so that now they were slick-skinned in some spots and hairy in others. The overall impression of the animals was that if there were any steep grades ahead, the passengers likely would have to get out and carry the mules.

As for other passengers waiting for this trip to commence, there seemed to be three, not counting Longarm, two men in business suits plus a lady who was hiding behind a wide-brimmed hat and heavy veil. And there was the driver, of course. Total of five humans going to Glory.

All of them, the driver included, were standing around like they were waiting for somebody to take charge, even though the stated departure time had come and then gone fifteen minutes ago.

Longarm was about to get peeved about it all. He'd slept poorly during the night, and then hadn't wanted to crawl out this morning. As it was he'd nearly overslept, and so had had to wolf his breakfast in order to get there on time. His stomach felt sour now because of that, full of undigested grease and coffee that'd tasted mostly of acid. And now they were all gonna stand around and wait?

"Mister," he said to the wagon driver, "are we gonna leave or aren't we?"

"We'll pull out direc'ly," the driver mumbled around a cud of tobacco.

"Before noon or after?" Longarm persisted.

The driver finally consented to turn his head and give the tall deputy a direct look. "Soon as the last passenger shows up, mister."

"I thought. . . ." After all, that dang clerk yesterday had pretty much implied a man had to be on time or get left behind until the next day. Well, sauce for one was sauce for all, wasn't it?

"Dammit, mister. 'Scuse me, ma'am," the wagon driver added with an apologetic bob of his head in the lady's direction. "What I'm saying, mister, is that we ain't gonna pull outta here till that last passenger is aboard. Not regardless. So's you might just as well calm down an' leave be."

Longarm sighed. The driver was right, of course. None of this was the driver's responsibility no matter what some clerk might've said, and there was no point whatsoever in Longarm getting his stomach churning over it. This railroad that did its business with mules and wagons instead of steam engines was entitled to act however it pleased. With or without Custis Long's consent. His snippiness now was just a carryover from last night. "Sorry," he said. "I only thought—"

"Yeah, I know, but this here passenger is different. One of the bosses, see. Owns a big piece of this here railroad line. Or what *will* be a railroad line by the end o' summer. So's you can see, I bet, why I'm gonna set here an' wait on the man long as it takes, mister. No matter how ruffled your feathers happen t' get." The driver grinned and spat.

"Sorry," Longarm repeated. He took a few steps away from the others and lighted a cheroot. The dry, clean flavor of the smoke tasted good and seemed to help settle him down. Longarm decided he was just being jumpy now because of what he could expect to face in Snowshoe. Every white in the country would despise the man who'd come to stand up for the hated Utes. Longarm could handle being an object of scorn and hatred. It wouldn't change a thing about what he thought or how he acted. But he didn't have to look forward to it or pretend to like it. Duty didn't go so far that it made a man less than human, and even a deputy U.S. marshal had feelings.

He grunted softly to himself. There he was, borrowing troubles that weren't in front of him. Why, he could think about all this when he got to Snowshoe. No point in fretting over it before then.

Once he'd given himself that little talking to, and had decided he could wait there cheerfully for however long it took, the last passenger arrived.

"All right, Jimmy, hurry it up. I don't have time to waste for the likes of you," the big boss snapped at the driver.

The man helped himself to a seat immediately behind the driving box, and gave everyone else impatient glares while the driver supervised the loading of several bags that a uniformed porter had carried in the big man's wake.

Longarm shrugged and helped the lady onto the wagon, then stepped off to the side to take a few last puffs on his cheroot before he got aboard. He frankly didn't give a damn what the other men might think of his smoke, but he wouldn't have considered getting on with a lighted cigar unless he checked with the lady first. The two businessmen, drummers presumably, got onto the wagon next, with Longarm finally trailing them and the driver climbing up last.

The lady sat across from the railroad boss. The drummers took up the bench in back, leaving Longarm a choice between planting himself next to the lady or beside the railroad boss. He chose to squeeze the railroad bigwig rather than force his presence on the woman.

The railroad boss was a large man. Not at all fat but definitely large. He was at least as tall as Longarm but probably was twice as broad. The fellow was middle-aged now, and certainly softer of body than he would once have been. Although anything harder than this guy now was would pretty much have to be classified as a metal, Longarm decided. He looked just plain solid.

And however he might have come to be where he now was, it hadn't been by shuffling papers from one drawer to another. The man's nose had been battered into a shape approximating that of a turnip, and there was scar tissue over both his eyes and across the knuckles on both his hands. If he hadn't been a professional pugilist he'd been one hell of a brawler.

The driver released his brake and clucked softly to the mules. The tough little animals tiptoed forward to take up the slack in the traces, then leaned into the load and began drawing the wagon along at a slow roll. It was a nice performance, Longarm noticed, accomplished without any lurch or jiggle. Very pleasant.

This was going to take a while, Longarm decided, so they might as well all be civilized to one another. He turned half around on the bench so he was more or less facing the railroad man. Longarm extended his hand and said, "Custis Long, sir. And you are . . . ?"

The railroader acted like he was all of a sudden smelling something that'd spoiled. He gave Longarm a cold, lengthy stare, then lifted his nose into the air and turned his head away without acknowledging the offered handshake.

Longarm chose not to make an issue of it. He sat back on his half of the seat and looked off in the other direction.

The railroader moved, jostling Longarm slightly as the big man reached inside his coat and pulled out a fat, expensive-looking pale-leaf cigar. He took his time about sniffing it, trimming it, wetting the wrapper leaf. Finally he clamped it between his lips and got out a match.

Without asking the lady's permission, Longarm noted.

The railroader scratched his lucifer aflame, and Longarm began to turn.

A slight motion of the woman's gloved hand got his attention. Longarm couldn't see her features behind the dark, heavy veil, but he could see the movement of her hat when she shook her head in a silent warning that he knew was intended for him. No, she was saying, don't make an issue of it.

Longarm grimaced. For his own satisfaction he might have wanted to. It might be kinda pleasant and personally rewarding to deliver a lesson in manners to this SOB. But that would only distress the lady, wouldn't it. And that wasn't at all what Longarm had in mind here. Darn it.

He grunted softly to himself and settled back into the corner of the seat bench again.

Chapter 6

"This is gonna take me a few minutes, folks. Got some fallen rock on the road, and I don't want to risk an axle going over it. So if anybody wants to stretch a bit or get a drink this is your chance." The driver set his brake and climbed down to begin the task of kicking chunks of stone out of the path. They had come to a halt on a flat, narrow ledge that ran between the creek they'd been following for the past half dozen miles and a steep, clifflike hillside above. It was from somewhere up there that the rock had fallen, partially blocking the way.

Longarm nodded to the lady and touched the brim of his Stetson. "Ma'am?"

"I am comfortable here, sir, thank you." Her voice was pleasant. Throaty and on the deep side for a woman, yet most definitely feminine. No doubt about that.

"Could I bring you a drink then?"

"That would be pleasant, thank you."

He touched his hat brim again and joined the two drummers in leaving the wagon. The railroad boss pulled another cigar out of his pocket, but made no effort to climb down to ground level where his smoke would not be so close to the veiled lady.

Longarm waited until he was clear before he pulled out a cheroot and allowed himself the pleasure of its flavor. He went around to the back of the wagon and reached into the luggage boot for his bag. He knew precisely where to find the article he wanted. It was . . . uh . . . he groped, grunted . . . there. He located it by feel and pulled it out.

The camp cup was a cunning little thing. It had been a gift. From a lady. But then cute, collapsible, silver camp cups, particularly ones with sentiments engraved on them, weren't exactly the sort of thing a man would buy for himself.

The cup consisted of a set of interlocking silver bands set one inside another and another and so on. Collapsed small for the purposes of carrying, the cup looked all the world like a circle of thick silver metal, yet one good shake and the rings would slide apart and lodge top to bottom to form a cylinder capable of holding eight or ten ounces of liquid. Clever, even if not as convenient as one's own palm when it came to drinking from mountain streams. Longarm opened it and gave it a tug to make sure the rings locked tight, then ambled over to the swift-running stream. The water was icy on his hand when he dipped the cup full, and before he was back to the wagon there was condensation forming on the outside of the metal cup. He walked around to the far side of the rig and handed the cup up rather than get back on board with his lighted cheroot.

"Thank you, sir."

"My pleasure, ma'am."

She had to lift her veil to drink, and he could see that this woman was what a man would hope to find behind every veil. Lovely. Her cheeks were rosy and full, her lips even rosier and more lush. Her eyes were dark and her lashes long and curling. She had dimples when she smiled. She wasn't any kid, being in her thirties at the least. Longarm didn't get a very good look at her. But good enough. He liked what he saw there. She drank quickly, holding her veil just barely aside while she did so, and then handed the empty cup back down to him. "Thank you, sir, I—"

"Hey!" the railroad boss barked. "You. It's, uh, don't tell me now." He snapped his fingers impatiently, the way some people will do in an effort to jog reluctant memory. "Dammit, I know you. Oh, hell, yes. Frenchie!" He barked out a laugh and leaned forward, one meaty hand probing

25

without warning or hesitation into the woman's crotch.

The lady cried out and shrank into a corner, but he had her trapped there. And his hand was searching now for the hem of her gown.

Longarm roared and swarmed the side of the wagon rather than wasting the time it would take to go around to the steps.

"You dumb son of a bitch," the railroader protested, "this is—"

He didn't have time enough to finish his statement. Longarm's right fist crushed his lips flat against his teeth, pulping soft flesh and sending blood flying.

The woman screamed and tried to draw away, but she was already trapped in a corner of the seat. There was nowhere she could go.

The man was no stranger to rough-and-tumble. And no single rap in the teeth was going to make him quit. Before Longarm was fully inside the wagon the railroader was responding with flying fists and elbows.

Longarm smothered the force of the blows by throwing himself on top of his adversary, wrestling the man off the woman and onto the floor of the wagon.

The two tussled there, neither able to get off any telling punches at such close quarters. Longarm was more or less on top of the railroader. Deliberately he drew back a little and got his legs under him while he waited for the powerfully built railroad boss to bull his way forward.

The railroader grunted and chopped, but at that range was doing nothing except to wear himself out. Longarm stayed close and waited.

As he expected, the railroader hadn't much patience and was used to having things all his own way. The man tried to dominate the situation by placing himself on top of the struggle.

Which was just what Longarm was wanting.

As soon as the railroader clawed himself nearly upright, Longarm launched himself at the man, driving with all his leg strength and using his forearms as battering rams. He caught the railroader low in the chest, coming up at the man from a low angle and driving through him.

The railroader flew backward. He hit the rim of the wagon box and was pushed over and beyond it, toppling out of the rig to fall heavily onto the hard gravel five feet below.

Longarm leaped after him, vaulting the side of the wagon and dropping knees first onto the railroader's gut.

The breath was driven out of the railroader, and he went pale. Longarm straddled the stricken man with one hand locked at the fellow's throat and his other fist upraised.

"I think," he gritted through clenched teeth, "you owe the lady an apology."

The railroader gave Longarm a look that was venomous. But he nodded meekly enough.

"Sorry I . . . bumped into you," Longarm said. He stood and helped the railroad boss to his feet, even turned the man around and helped brush off his backside. "Now," Longarm said. "I believe there was somethin' you were gonna say t' the lady?"

The railroad man scowled and looked like he was willing to seek a second opinion, then for some reason thought better of it. He cleared his throat, bowed in the direction of the wagon where the veiled woman was watching, and made a stiffly awkward apology that sounded every bit as insincere as it no doubt was. Still, insincere or not, it satisfied the proprieties.

"An honest error, I am sure," the lady said graciously, then looked away as if to pretend that none of it had ever happened.

The railroad man gave Longarm a murderous look but said nothing. He picked up the hat that he'd lost in the tussle, then climbed back onto the wagon and went to the rear, taking the seat that the two drummers had shared until now. Longarm gathered that the seating arrangements were changing for the remainder of the journey.

The businessmen, who had been staying well out of the way while all this went on, boarded the wagon again too and occupied the bench that until now Longarm and the railroader had used. Longarm's choice for the rest of the trip would be in the back beside the railroad boss or else in the middle beside the lady.

The lady said nothing, but she did simplify the decision for him by sliding over to the side of her seat and ostentatiously holding her skirts aside to make room there.

"Ready, mister?" the driver asked. He too seemed to be pretending that nothing had happened during the halt.

"Yes, thank you." Longarm got back on and sat beside the woman. He could feel the warmth of her thigh close beside his leg. The seat benches were narrow on this rig. But not *that* narrow. He smiled and touched the brim of his hat to her again.

She handed him an object that at first he couldn't identify. What it looked like was a piece of trash, a twig or bit of half-rotted bark that someone might find littering a forest floor. Then he realized that this crushed and splintered thing was what remained of the cheroot he'd been smoking when he invaded the wagon. He had quite forgotten it.

"I enjoy the fragrance of a gentleman's cigar," she said, placing a distinct emphasis on the word "gentleman's" loudly enough for the railroader on the bench behind them to overhear. And again Longarm was acutely aware of the warmth of her body so close beside his.

"Thank you, ma'am," he said solemnly as he pulled out a fresh cheroot and began the rituals of tending to it.

Longarm found himself hoping that the lady was on her way through to Snowshoe just like he was.

Chapter 7

It was past noon when the wagon reached the end of the railroad tracks where they could pick up the narrow-gauge line into Glory. It peeved Longarm that there was no provision made for box lunches for the passengers. He himself could get along fine without a meal, but the railroad should have been more considerate of the lady he was traveling beside. She shouldn't be expected to travel all day without food.

Traveling beside, he reflected, but certainly not traveling with. The lady hadn't spoken again since that stop back along the way. But Longarm hadn't exactly been able to forget about her. By the time they reached the transfer point at the track-end, she was sitting so that her leg was pressed tight against his. As he was by now uncomfortably aware. All that jostling contact had had him in a state of erection for much of the trip, damn it, and there was nothing he could do to relieve the problem.

Even so, it was with mixed feelings on the subject that Longarm climbed down and helped the lady to the ground after first allowing the railroader and the drummers to leave.

By then the driver was already transferring luggage to a crudely built platform near the timbered bumper that had been constructed to block the cars from rolling off the end of the track. Longarm stayed with the lady just in case the shit-for-brains railroad boss was waiting to catch her without a protector nearby.

The railroader was glaring first at his pocket watch and then down the tracks in the direction of Glory. Apparently the train that was to meet them was late in arriving at this end. Longarm wouldn't have wanted to be in the shoes of that engine crew when the boss got done with them tonight. The man didn't look at all happy about being kept waiting there.

"We made good time," the wagon driver offered. "The train isn't due for another fifteen, twenty minutes, sir."

The boss gave the driver a nasty look that shut the poor man up right quick. Apparently that train was due when the boss damned well wanted it, not when the crew previously had been told to be there, Longarm guessed. Nice guy.

The wagon driver, who really had done an excellent job, quickly finished unloading the luggage from his rig, then climbed back onto his driving box and wheeled the team of small but tough little mules without waiting to give his animals a breather. He touched the brim of his cap and pulled away almost immediately, leaving the would-be train passengers standing alone in the mountain wilderness. Longarm would have been willing to place a sizable wager that most days the driver would have stayed until the train arrived. And that he wouldn't be much more than out of sight from there before he stopped again and rested his team now.

"You don't happen to see a, um, comfort facility close by, do you?" the lady whispered to him, probably distressed now that the wagon driver was gone and no one else there would likely know anything about the services the railroad line provided. Or failed to.

"I'll look around." Longarm walked up to the platform and checked. There were no signs in place there to show the way to any rest rooms, and certainly there were no outhouses visible. There was, however, a barely visible path beaten into the brush at trackside. Maybe that led to a sink or cat hole anyway. He went back and got the lady and guided her to the start of the path. "This way, ma'am."

The path proved to be a disappointment, though. It led not to a latrine but to a barren patch of gravel beside the creek that had carved this canyon they were in.

30

"Sorry, ma'am. But at least there's some brush between here an' the platform. If you, uh, wanta put up with, um, primitive conditions."

"I am afraid I have no choice, Mr. Longarm."

"Ma'am?" His confusion arose because he hadn't told her his name. Nor, for that matter, had he been given hers.

"Forgive me if I've offended you. It was written on your cup."

"Oh, yes." He'd forgotten. The engraving. "Longarm from Jessica, with Love." And a date that had only private meaning.

"Is it a pet name that I should avoid?" she asked.

"No, just a nickname my friends use. An' you're welcome to too."

"Then so I shall, Mr. Longarm."

"Not mister, just plain Longarm, okay?"

"As you wish. I am Leah Skelde."

"Miss Skelde." He bowed to her.

"Just plain Leah would be friendlier, Longarm."

"My pleasure, Leah." He bowed again.

"May I ask a favor of you, Longarm?"

"Anything within reason."

"Then turn your back, please, while I make a dash for those bushes over there."

He laughed. Now that she was speaking he liked her all the more. She acted like a lady, but could talk blunt and honest too. "I think that's within reason, Leah." He touched his Stetson to her and turned his back. He could hear her scurry away into the brush to relieve herself.

There wasn't anything to do but stare straight ahead, which happened to be in the direction of the mountain stream and the hillside opposite it. Leah took long enough peeing that Longarm got a very good look at that bit of empty country.

A mildly odd little bit it was too, once he thought about it.

There was the fact that a path led down there to begin with. Not that it was much of a path, and it sure hadn't been used very often. Still, he could see where people had passed back and forth along it for no obvious purpose.

Yet when he looked closer he could see that there were some flat stones laid in the creek bed. Creating a sort of ford there? He couldn't be sure.

And on the hillside opposite him there was a place that looked kind of like an avalanche chute, an area where it looked like rock had fallen, gouging the red earth bare like a footpath, except much, much too steep there for anything, even a goat, to walk. But much too narrow for it to be a winter avalanche zone. Those were always fairly broad and easily spotted from miles away. This was much smaller than that. And anyway, there wasn't any rock scree nor fallen timbers at the base of the hillside to account for it being an avalanche site.

Odd, Longarm thought.

He might have suspected it was a path used by prospectors leaving the train at the end-of-track platform, except that it was so steep. Couldn't be any sort of path, he concluded.

What it came right down to, he finally determined, was that he had no idea what in hell could've caused it. Or why.

He quit pondering it when he heard Leah's footsteps approaching him from behind. She came up beside him and linked her arm into his.

"I'm impressed, Longarm. You didn't peek even once." Her veil was thrown back, and this time he could get a good look at her. The sight had been worth waiting for. She was even prettier than he'd thought.

"Reckon I'm a little too old t' be satisfied with a glimpse o' petticoat, Leah."

Her smile turned into a grin, and that into a laugh. "Oh, Longarm. You can't know."

"Know what, Leah?"

"How hard it was for me to keep from laughing before. In that wagon. When you were riding so stern and serious and trying not to admit that you had a tent pole stuck behind your fly."

"You . . . ?"

"Have I shocked you, Longarm? I apologize. Sort of."
She gave him an impish grin and squeezed his elbow. "But
I couldn't not see a thing that huge, could I?"

"You aren't. . . ."

"Everything I seem to be? No. But I'm not everything I
once was either."

"Now I'm more confused than before," he admitted.

"I only brought it up so I could explain, dear Longarm.
You see, the gentleman on the coach may well have
remembered me from before. And I did indeed use a
great many names. And do a great many things that I
probably shouldn't have done. It is entirely possible that
he has fucked me in the past, Longarm. Or wanted to and
couldn't afford me then, which is somewhat more likely
since I don't remember him at all. I was expensive, you
see. I was the very best if I do say so myself. Now all of
that is behind me. Now I am an investor and sometimes
a saloon keeper and gaming-hall proprietor. But nobody,
Longarm, *nobody* ever comes into my bed nowadays except
by invitation." She squeezed his elbow again. "You are a
lovely man, Longarm. Consider yourself invited."

"I dunno about bein' a lovely man," he said with a
chuckle, "but I'd sure have t' say that I'm a lucky one."

Leah smiled and came onto her tiptoes to give him
a brief hint of what her invitation entailed. Her mouth
found his, and her tongue darted and flickered. She tasted
faintly of mint and perhaps other spices as well, and her
scent was that of spring wildflowers. There was no way
to judge her figure, hidden as it was behind the padding
of a gown stiff enough and heavy enough to withstand the
rigors of hard travel. But her body was certainly plenty
warm enough. Longarm's erection was returning at double
strength.

"Later," she whispered huskily into his mouth. Then, the
promise delivered, she pulled away. She drew the veil back
over her pretty face and once more seemed a remote and
proper gentlewoman.

33

The sudden gusts and eddies of sensation this woman could cause or as quickly withdraw were positively disorienting. Longarm felt himself sway unsteadily, and might actually have staggered a bit if it hadn't been for Leah's grip on his elbow. Then she was gone, walking ahead of him up the path toward the platform and the other travelers just as prim as prim could be.

Longarm shook his head as if to clear it of a sudden fog, and hurried to catch up with her.

Chapter 8

It was mid-afternoon—a little past mid-afternoon, actually—before the narrow-gauge puffer dragged into Glory with a wood car, four flatcars, and one passenger coach in tow.

Late enough, Longarm decided, that it would be foolish to start off again immediately on the final leg of his trip to Snowshoe. Better, he thought, to wait until morning so he could be sure of finding the way.

As the few passengers were disembarking onto the Glory depot's small platform, he noticed that the railroad boss was being met by a delegation of men wearing starched collars and long faces. Their expressions seemed even stiffer than their batwing collars, Longarm thought. He had the impression that these people were waiting for news that would be vitally important to them. And that the idiot railroad man was the one who was bringing that information, perhaps even was responsible for it, judging from the way everyone fawned over him once he stepped onto the platform.

Whatever that was about, though, it wasn't something a deputy marshal had to worry about. Longarm helped the lady down the portable steps to the firm planking, then directed a porter with a hand truck to collect her luggage and his own few things. They would, after all, be stopping at the same hotel.

"Ah, yes," the clerk at the Grand said after poring over his ledger. "I have it here, reservation in the name of L. K. Skelde." He gave the veiled woman a questioning look. But then it wasn't really common for a woman to be traveling alone on business. The man transferred his attention to Longarm. "And you, sir, would be wanting an, um, adjoining accommodation?"

"I'll be wantin' an accommodation," Longarm said coldly. "I don't recollect saying nothing about where in the hotel it oughta be."

"My mistake, sir, ma'am." The clerk hurriedly bent to his ledger once again. He called a bellboy to carry Leah's luggage to Room 27 and handed Longarm the key to Room 14. "I hope you both enjoy your stay."

Longarm waited downstairs a few minutes to enjoy a cheroot and a glass of a middling-fair rye—he didn't want to seem in too great a hurry to get up those stairs—then wandered up to his room. Number 14 was on the second floor of the narrow, boxy hotel building; 27 was on the top floor one flight up.

Longarm stopped in his own room only long enough to drop his things on the foot of the bed, take his hat off, and give his hair a quick slicking back. Then he was out again and striding for the staircase.

He tapped lightly on the door. "Miss Skelde? I believe this might be yours?" Just in case someone was listening.

"It's open. Come in."

Longarm let himself into the room. And stopped immediately, a quick smile tugging at his lips.

"Bolt the door, won't you please, dear?"

He found the bolt by feel and slid it home. He didn't want to take his eyes off Leah. Not yet.

The heavy travel gown was gone, discarded somewhere out of sight already. So were the hat and the veil.

Leah stood before him now wearing only her foundation garments: corset, pantaloons, garter belt, silk stockings, high-top shoes. Her honey-brown hair was piled high and pinned in a mass of tight curls. She wore a cameo brooch on a ribbon tied tight at her throat and matching cameo earbobs.

She was . . . mouth-watering. Exquisite. Statuesque.

36

Her waist was impossibly narrow, her hips and legs slim and sleek. Her bosom swelled high and sharp and proud over a taut expanse of flat belly, and the texture of her skin was that of fresh-whipped cream.

"Do you like it?"

"I like it," he admitted.

Leah smiled and turned in a slow and deliberately provocative pirouette so he could see and assess her from all sides.

"Yeah," he said. "I like it."

"Do you want to undress me, dear?"

"You go ahead. I think I'll watch." He crossed the room to the one armchair that was provided and settled into it. He brought out a cheroot and lighted it, taking his time about it and giving the smoke most of his attention for the moment. Finally he stuck the cigar in his jaw at a jaunty angle, crossed his legs, and gave Leah the nod. "Now I'm set t' appreciate you proper."

She half turned away from him and glanced briefly over a creamy shoulder as if to satisfy herself that he was still watching. Then she lifted one foot onto the side of the bed and leaned forward to begin unlacing her shoe. One shoe and then the other were slowly removed. She had fine legs. And a superb back as well, Longarm saw. She was sleek as an otter, with no spare flesh on her but with an abundance of absolutely everything that she needed.

She twisted, turned, posed for his benefit while pretending to act like a lady alone in her boudoir. After the shoes the stockings went. Then the corset laces.

Leah needed no corset to slim her waist, he saw. But she certainly needed help containing those magnificent breasts. They fairly leaped into view as the halves of the corset dropped away. Her tits were pale melons of proud flesh tipped with delicate pink. Despite their size they sagged only a little.

Leah paused in her show and winked at him. By now she wore only the garter belt and pantaloons. The garter belt went next. She hooked her thumbs into the elasticized

37

cloth and wriggled, stepping out of the skeletal garment and kicking it aside.

"Well, dear?"

Longarm smiled. "Everything," he said. "I do want it all, Leah."

She laughed, obviously enjoying the desire she could see in his eyes. Then she pushed the pantaloons down and kicked them off too. She was naked now save for the cameo jewelry.

"Perfect," he said.

And so she was. Her pubis was as naked as her belly, shaven for some reason. Whatever that reason, Longarm liked the effect. On Leah this essentially unnatural change somehow made her body seem all one piece, one long, flowing, glorious work of art.

But warm art. And malleable.

Longarm stood and stubbed his cheroot out in a china dish. He beckoned, and Leah rushed to him. Pressed herself against him and lifted her mouth to his.

Her breath was warm and her tongue insistent. Her body molded itself gently to his. The jut of the erection that was trapped behind his fly bridged what little gap there was between them and prodded the softness of Leah's belly.

He ran his hands up and down her back. She trembled and twisted in a slow, sensuous, involuntary dance, undulating beneath his touch like some great tawny cat wanting to be petted and fondled.

She pulled her lips back from his just enough to give her room to whisper, yet close enough that he could feel the movement of her mouth gently tickle him when she spoke. "Close your eyes, darling, and I'll make this a night you'll never forget."

"It ain't night yet," he pointed out.

Leah smiled. "It will be, dear, before your breathing comes back to normal."

"Mmm?"

"Guaranteed, darling. Why, I daresay I shall have you so limp and ruined that you'll not be able to walk out of here before midnight. It won't be until tomorrow that you return to normal."

"Pretty lady, you an' I both know that such a thing ain't humanly possible. But I sure got t' admire your spunk. If awards are ever given out for ambition, I bet you take first prize."

Leah chuckled and pressed her face to his for a moment, sucking Longarm's lower lip into her mouth and running her tongue back and forth across it. She wriggled her belly against the bulge of his cock and hugged him. "Sweetheart, you only *think* I'm exaggerating."

"Honey, this here is one time I'd admire t' be proved wrong. And one thing sure. I won't do nothing t' stop you from trying. So have you at it, ma'am. I am yours t' drain dry." He threw his head back and his arms wide in surrender, and closed his eyes as Leah had requested.

"Longarm, dear, you simply can't know how much fun this is going to be for both of us. But I'm glad you are willing to find out." She laughed again, and he felt the butterfly-light touch of her fingers tugging delicately at the buttons and buckles of his clothing.

Chapter 9

Longarm stretched, his teeth chattering as he contained a yawn. Damn, but he felt whipped. No doubt Leah did too. But, Lordy, she was one helluva woman. She could turn a man inside out and then wring him dry. Which Custis Long certainly was at the moment.

What he needed now, he figured, was a stiff drink— wasn't anything else about him likely to be stiff again for a long while—and a full night's sleep. At least that part should be easy enough to come by. It wasn't hardly past dark yet.

"Where you goin', Leah?" he asked as he felt her slide off the bed.

"Mmm, you'll see, darling." She sounded playful and still quite fresh even though she'd bucked and shuddered through her own powerful climaxes just as frequently as he had over the past several hours.

"C'mon back t' bed an' lemme sleep," he mumbled. He rolled over and buried his face in one of the feather pillows. "Blow out the lamp when you come back, willya?"

Distantly he could hear Leah puttering around in the room. He could hear her footsteps, the click of crockery on china, the spill of water from the pitcher into a bowl. There was a pause, and then some other noises that he couldn't quite identify beyond realizing that they had something to do with the water she'd just poured. Oh, well. He began to drift toward sleep, began to feel almost weightless, as if he were severing the connections with his own body and was starting to float free above the rumpled, sweaty bed. The sensation was pleasant.

Leah returned to the bed. He sensed her presence standing over him. Not on her own side at all but standing on his side of the bed. Then she sat beside him. He could feel the mattress depress.

"Mmm-gumphhh."

Leah laughed.

"Hey!" Longarm came upright with a leap as something cold and wet blanketed his face and damned near smothered him.

"It's all right, dear," Leah soothed, pulling the washcloth away. She grinned. "Surely you didn't think you were going to go to sleep on me so soon, darling. Why, we've barely begun here."

"You can't mean that," he said.

"But of course I can. Trust me." She pushed on his chest, guiding him back down onto the bed. She bathed his face and neck with the wet, chilly cloth, then plumped the pillow behind his neck. "Trust me," she repeated with a smile.

"You woke me up," he said accusingly.

"But of course, darling. How else could I make this lovely thing hard again so we can fuck some more? Gracious, dear, you'd be no use to me asleep. Now would you?" she asked in a gay, teasing voice. She bent forward again, bathing his throat and upper chest. "Trust me."

"Oh, I do that well enough, I s'pose. But you're flogging a dead horse if you think you can get another rise outta that limp thing down there. You've plumb worn it out, honey, and I won't get no more use out of it, nor you won't neither, until I've had some rest here. Which is what I was tryin' t' do when you went an' woke me up."

"Trust me," she insisted.

Longarm shrugged and made no effort to stop her.

Leah dunked the washcloth into the basin to wet it again, and twisted most of the fresh, really quite cold water out of it. She washed his chest and stomach. "Does that feel nice?"

41

"So-so," he said. "Mostly it just wakes me up."

"Trust me."

She bathed his cock and balls perfunctorily, spending no more time there than she had on his belly, then moved on to his legs and his feet. She took her time washing between his toes, much more time there in fact than she had on his pecker. He wasn't at all interested in screwing again and wouldn't be for hours, but even so he found that imbalance of attention slightly disconcerting. If nothing else, though, he conceded, he was damn sure awake now. Her attentions had certainly done that much.

"Roll over, dear."

He did as she asked, and Leah bathed the backs of his legs, then moved up beside his head and started down his neck and back. Finally only his butt remained unwashed. He started to roll onto his back again, but Leah stopped him.

"Not yet, dear."

"I know. Trust you."

"Exactly," she said cheerfully. He could hear her dipping the cloth in the basin again, and then she began cheerfully washing his ass. "Perfectly clean all over," she said when she was finally done.

"Well, I'm glad you're happy 'bout it. Can I go t' sleep now?"

"Longarm! Really! Tru—"

"Trust me," he said, finishing the often-repeated phrase in unison with her.

Leah patted him, and left the bedside to return the basin and cloth to the washstand in the corner. She came back to the bed and stood there for a moment while she unpinned her hair and let it fly loose with a shake of her pretty head. "Close your eyes, darling. No, don't roll over, please. I want you on your stomach. I'll tell you when to change. Thank you, dear."

Longarm was wide awake now. And mildly curious as to what Leah had in mind even though he wasn't at all interested in getting it up again yet.

He felt nothing. Heard nothing. Leah might have left the room, except he would have heard her if she'd moved. What the hell, he decided. Maybe he could go to sleep now after all. Then he felt . . . moth wings fluttering above him? A cool and gentle breeze? What? It was so light, so delicate that he wasn't honestly sure. At first he couldn't even be positive that he was feeling anything at all. Then . . .

Leah moved, and the tip ends of her hair brushed softly over his back and down to his waist. Barely in contact at first, then more fully so that he could feel and identify what she was doing.

The sensation was interesting. Not arousing, certainly, but interesting in an odd sort of way. He yawned.

The touch of her hair became firmer as she bent lower. Then another sensation was added to it somewhere in the vicinity of his shoulder blades. Something warm. And moist. Her tongue, he decided. Yeah, he could feel it now. She was licking his back. It kinda tickled. And then went away completely. He was getting sleepy again now. Might have t' go to sleep now even if Leah did want him t' try again. Might have to . . .

She began licking the back of his neck. Behind his ears and inside them. Then down onto one shoulder and across to the other. Down his spine to the small of his back. Lower onto his ass.

He realized what she was doing now. Leah was bathing him again. But this time with her tongue. Felt nice too. He yawned, a little more awake again now than he really wanted to be.

Then he blinked and came wide awake of a sudden.

Leah sure as hell wasn't a shy girl. She'd cleaned him up first. Now her tongue was following everywhere that washcloth had gone. Right on into the crack of his ass. And staying there in some right serious explorations. Damn!

He could feel the press of her pretty face between the cheeks of his ass, could feel the tip of her tongue circle and probe, dipping lightly inside a fraction of an inch and back out again.

43

She began to suck on him and moan.

And now she was lying partially on top of him with her arms circling his waist and her hands finding his cock and his balls.

She kneaded his prick with one hand and cupped his balls in the warmth of the other while still she continued to suck and tongue his asshole.

Longarm felt completely surrounded by womanflesh. Engulfed inside Leah Skelde. Captured totally within her. The experience was unusual. But not at all unpleasant.

He felt his cock engorge and thicken, felt the warmly encouraging pull of her fingers and the hot probing of her tongue.

He gasped and lifted his hips off the bed in an effort to help her.

"Lie still, darling. Keep your eyes closed and lie still. I'll move you when we're ready, dear. Lie still, dear, and let me take you out of yourself more completely than you've ever known before. Just lie quiet and let me consume you, darling. Trust me."

Longarm let go of his last shreds of resistance. He kept his eyes closed and allowed his entire body, save for that one small portion, to be limp and quiescent.

He was still engulfed by her. He felt like he was floating. At this point he no longer knew—or cared—which part of Leah was doing what to him. He only knew that he was lifted and supported and surrounded by the warmth that was Leah. Only knew that he was welling full of sensation. Full of seed. So full that he overflowed with it and his fluids spilled slowly out. Flowed, not jetted, out of him and into her. Flowed for what seemed a very long, very lovely time.

He felt the contractions of Leah's throat and felt the clasp of her lips around the base of his cock, and recognized without minding in the slightest that somehow sometime she had moved so that now her hands massaged his ass while it was her mouth that contained his pecker. At this moment he didn't even find it odd that she could have

44

made that change without him noticing. But then he'd been so completely surrounded by her that the details hadn't mattered. Hadn't and still didn't.

Longarm sighed and realized that he was no longer oozing cum into her mouth even though the ducts that carried the fluid through him felt like they remained open. That seemed a strange sensation, and not a particularly pleasant one. He sure hell was empty now, though. As completely empty as he'd ever been in his life, and maybe then some. Damn! He smiled and lay there with his eyes closed, his cock again limp but still held warm and secure within Leah's mouth while her hands supported his balls and lay gently on the rim of his asshole.

He should say something to her. He knew he really should. Congratulate her. Thank her. Some damn thing. He sighed again. He really would too. Just as soon as he woke up. Longarm felt himself floating, drifting, receding happily into a gentle darkness.

And then he felt nothing at all.

Chapter 10

Longarm lay propped up on both pillows while Leah rested in the crook of his arm with her cheek pressed against his chest. He had a cheroot in one hand and her right tit in the other. All in all he would have admitted to being downright content at this particular moment.

It was, he guessed, somewhere around five in the morning, and he was feeling fine. He'd had a good night's sleep thanks to the early start last night, and had just finished enjoying Leah's body once more. Now he had a cigar going. Hell, it didn't get much better. And if he was ravenously hungry after skipping supper, well, that was what restaurants and cafes were for. He could go downstairs and take care of all that soon enough.

"Can I tell you something, Longarm?" Leah whispered.

"O' course."

"I don't want to sound silly. I mean, you aren't some wet-behind-the-ears schoolboy. You're smart enough and man enough to understand that whores lie, dear. A sensible gentleman never believes a word a whore tells him because it's all a hustle. All she ever wants is his money."

"Is this takin' us somewhere, Leah?"

"Yes. I just . . . I'm not in the business now, dear, but I used to be. I don't pretend otherwise. I mean, I was the best. Top prices and top performance and no apologies asked nor given. You understand that?"

He nodded.

"Well, all I'm trying to say, dear . . . all I want you to know . . . you are a very special man, Longarm. And I've enjoyed being with you. That's all I want you to know. But it isn't a lie, darling. It isn't any kind of a lie, and if you think that it is, well . . ."

He laughed. "Will you shut up and stop worrying?"

"But if you think that is just another lie from just another whore, dear . . ."

"You said what you had t' say. Now let me say something back, okay?"

She nodded solemnly.

"Thank you. Thank you for the compliment an' thank you for last night. An' that's all I got t' say on the subject."

Leah smiled and seemed satisfied. She touched his face and then nuzzled his side in contentment. "Will I see you again tonight, dear?"

"Wish we could, but I gotta get on. Goin' to a place called Snowshoe."

"I've heard of it. In fact, I'll be going there myself soon. I've come to investigate all these new boom camps. I'll open a business in at least one of them, possibly two if I can find a reliable manager. You, um, wouldn't be looking for work, would you, dear?"

He laughed and shook his head. "Not me. I got all the work I can handle at the moment, but I thank you." It occurred to him that he never had exactly gotten around to telling her what kind of work it was that he did. He saw no reason to change that at this late date.

"Will you be in Snowshoe long?"

He shrugged.

"If you're still there when I arrive . . . ?"

"Then I'll be wanting to hook up with you again, you bet. You're a fine woman, Leah. A pleasure t' be with. An' I don't mean just in bed. You're nice company. So quit down-talkin' yourself. Anything you used t' do got nothing t' do with here and now. You hear me?"

She smiled and nodded and kissed his chest. "If you are still there, dear, and if you still want me . . ."

"I'll be counting on it," he said.

"Good."

"Reckon I'd best be sneaking back t' my own room now. Wouldn't want anybody getting the wrong idea about you." He gave her a hug. "Besides, I oughta get more use out o' that room than just storage for my things. At the least I can muss up the bed and do my shaving there."

"I don't want you to go," she said.

"Got to. But I'll see you in Snowshoe."

"Please don't leave before I get there, dear. If you have to, at least leave a message for me. Where I can find you? I'd . . . I'd go anywhere to be with you, Longarm. Isn't that perfectly silly of me? Why, a hard-hearted old bawd like me, you'd think I would be past the moon-eyed stage of falling for some handsome ne'er-do-well."

"Are you tryin' to call me a—"

"No! Oh, please don't think that, darling, please don't. It's me who's being so awful, not you. But it's true, dear. I would follow you anywhere, do anything for you. Give you money, be your slave, go back to selling my ass to keep you in the chips, anything you like. It's true. And I don't know a thing about you. Not really."

The crazy damn woman was carrying this kind of far in Longarm's opinion. After all, a night of bounce and tickle was one thing. But no matter how damned good it was— and in Leah's case it damn sure had been plenty good—a night of belly-bumping was all it'd been. And all he wanted it to be.

Better, he decided, if he could get his business in Snowshoe wrapped up quick so he could be gone again before Leah got around to joining him there.

"We'll talk 'bout all that in Snowshoe," he told her.

"Promise?"

"Absolutely," he lied. He kissed her on the forehead, then left the bed and began dragging his clothes back on.

By the time he was back in his own room he had all but forgotten Leah.

Chapter 11

"I'm real sorry, mister, but you can't hardly get to that place from here," the railroad clerk said apologetically.

Longarm tipped his Stetson back and frowned. "But I'm sure the man in Silver Creek told me I could reach Snowshoe by way of Glory."

"What he maybe didn't tell you, mister, is that our rail line and theirs are on completely different levels. Run close together part of the way, but they're real different. We've been building down low along the bottoms. They're bridging and boring and building high. The two lines never do come together. Don't now and never will."

"He told me that," Longarm persisted, "but he also said from Glory I should be able to get transportation up to the, oh, whatever the hell the name of that other railroad is, get up there to it anyway and take a train the rest of the way in to Snowshoe."

"The Bitterroot and Brightwater is the name of their line," the clerk helpfully supplied.

"Right, that was it."

"But you can't get there from here," the man insisted. "We don't have any connection with them and we don't plan one. Honestly."

"You're talking about a rail connection," Longarm said.

The clerk gave him a blank look. "Certainly."

"But I could walk up and make a connection, couldn't I?"

"Walk? Climb would be more like it." The man sniffed. Loudly. Walking? Climbing? On one's own feet? In the

49

mountains? Surely a man would have to be daft to even think of such a notion. He sniffed again.

"But I could do it?" Longarm hadn't come here to screw the pretty women of Glory. He'd come down here, dammit, with a job to do. In Snowshoe.

The clerk sniffed and refused to answer such a patently silly question.

Longarm thanked the fellow for all his help and ambled outside, where he stood in the slanting early morning sunlight and lighted a cheroot.

A few questions put to a passing railroad brakeman, though, assured him that not everyone in the town of Glory mistook convenience for necessity. This man, a dark-haired little fellow with gaps in his teeth and a happy lilt to his voice, seemed to think it perfectly acceptable that someone might want to walk, climb, or crawl about the countryside without benefit of upholstered benches and dining car service. "Sure thing, mister. Easy t' get there. Just you follow these tracks back toward the rail-end for, oh, four or five miles till you can look up an' spot another grade up 'bove you. Then just pick you a spot an' climb up. Don't know for sure where their rail-end is right now, but they'd got that far along in their construction when they laid off for the weather last fall. Mayhap e'en all the way through t' Snowshoe."

"Is that why neither line is building right now?" Longarm asked. "They still haven't commenced the spring work yet?"

"Me, I'm just a day-money hired man, neighbor. I ain't paid to do no heavy thinking," the brakeman said. "But anybody can see right plain that the weather's broke a month ago an' better. That makes for an excuse 'bout not having no construction crews yet, but it ain't no reason. What I hear is that we've run outta money. An' that Bitterroot an' Brightwater line too, else I'd be up there lookin' for a job. Hell, I'll go you one idea more. If anybody was t' ask me, which nobody has, I'd say that won't very many o' these camps survive long if they can't get rails in to 'em."

"No?"

50

"No, sir, an' I'll tell you why. The veins here run vertical. Takes a lotta gear an' a lotta money to mine straight up an' down. Whole lot more expensive than horizontal digging because you got to lift everything out a bit at a time. That makes it slow as well as hard. Worse, there's a lotta water seepage in the deep shafts, so that has t' be pumped out too, an' it's no easier to lift water than it is t' lift gold ore. It takes heavy equipment t' mine this country, neighbor. Big pumps, steam engines, fast hoists . . . all that stuff is easy enough t' move on a railroad car, but damn difficult t' carry on a mule's back."

"You sound like a man who knows what he's talking about."

The brakeman nodded solemnly and accepted the cheroot Longarm offered. He struck his own light and inhaled the smoke with obvious pleasure, holding it deep for a moment and smiling before he spoke again. "Thanks. That's fine. An' yessir, I know a thing or two 'bout hauling and 'bout mining too. I been a bullwhacker an' a freighter an' a powder monkey above ground an' below it too. I've hauled light rails by mule train, an' then turned right around an' laid those rails inside mine adits t' make track for ore carts. Then even hired on t' work in one of those same mines an' filled carts on track I'd just got done layin' down. Yessir, I expect I do know a few things 'bout this country an' what it takes to make a living in it."

"And you don't think Snowshoe or any of these other camps will make it?"

"That ain't exactly what I said. Any of 'em can make it, I think. *If* they get the rails through so's they can bring the proper equipment in an' get their ores out at a reasonable cost. That's one o' the things about these camps, see. The ones farthest out get the shit end o' the stick every way possible. Can't get equipment in t' set up mills an' refineries that'd reduce the raw ore to something light an' manageable. Can't afford to haul raw ore out to have it refined elsewhere. That's 'cause it costs, say, ten dollars t' haul a ton of ore. Costs, say, another ten dollars to get

51

that ore outta the ground. And on top of everything else you got to pay to have your ore processed. An' if a ton o' ore is only yielding, say, fifteen dollars, well, you tell me how long a man can stay in business that way."

"But if a railroad comes in . . . ?"

"Then you can bring in the equipment that lets you get your ore outta the ground for maybe six dollars a ton 'stead of ten. An' you put in your own mill an' process your ore right on the spot at a cost of maybe a dollar a ton 'stead of paying good money to haul it elsewhere. What all that means is that your same mine, same ore, same deal all around is earning you eight dollars a ton 'stead of costing you five or six."

"You ever think about being a businessman?" Longarm asked.

"Me?" The grease-stained brakeman laughed. "I ain't smart enough for that, mister. Me, I'm just a easy-going ol' boy with a broad back an' no brains. Ask anybody. Draw my wages the end o' every day an' drink 'em up every night. That's all I want outta life, neighbor. That an' to be left alone." He inspected the glowing tip of his cheroot, then added with a wink, "An' to have me a good smoke now an' again. For which I thank you."

"I've enjoyed talking to you, friend," Longarm said, meaning it.

"Any time," the cheerful little day laborer said as he went on his way.

Longarm figured it was time for him to get along on his way too. He went back to the hotel for breakfast, and as a precaution asked the dining room to make him up a box lunch, then went up to his virtually unused hotel room to reclaim his gear and carry everything down. By that time the box lunch was waiting for him. He paid for it and tucked it into his bag.

He hadn't even started out yet, but already he was grumbling under his breath.

This wasn't the sort of country, nor the sort of trip through it, that would lend itself comfortably to a man traveling with luggage and a saddle.

Yet there would be no point in trying to hire a saddle horse. Even if one was available—and that wasn't real likely in a mining camp like this—he probably would only have to abandon it in a few miles anyway. He hadn't been paying all that much attention to the hillsides while he was on that train yesterday, but what he did see wasn't country that would be easily covered from horseback. This was country where a man was apt to require good handholds and a keen sense of balance.

And now he was having to tackle it with a saddle in one hand and a suitcase in the other?

Longarm scowled. He also set out walking down the railroad tracks, though, awkward encumbrances or no. The sooner he got started, the sooner the ordeal would be done with. And the sooner those Utes would benefit from the writ of habeas corpus Lawyer Able had managed to scare up for them.

That, after all, was what this nuisance was all about.

Chapter 12

Hell, Longarm thought as he walked into Snowshoe, this hadn't been half as bad as he'd expected. The going had been slow but not particularly difficult. Not even getting from the Silver Creek, Tipson, and Glory tracks up to the level of the Bitterroot and Brightwater. That had just been a matter of picking a likely spot to climb, and then going slow and easy on the way up.

Except for that little distance, though, the journey had been a flat, boring hike along graded and ballasted railroad rights of way, walking the tracks of first the one line and then the other.

Longarm would have actually enjoyed the fresh air and exercise if it hadn't been for having to carry his bag and saddle. Toting those hadn't been especially fun. His shoulders ached now from the day-long strain, and his hands were just the least bit sore. But there wasn't anything that a drink and a good supper wouldn't cure, he figured.

He didn't have a hand free to pull his watch out and check the time, but his belly told him it was coming supper time. That impression was reinforced by the chill in the evening breeze. At this altitude the days might be nice and warm so long as the sun was shining, but the nights were cold the whole year round, and evening shadows could drive a chill into a man's bones. The sun had slid down beneath the westerly peaks the better part of an hour ago now, and the daylight was commencing to slowly, almost imperceptibly diminish like a lamp with the wick being eased lower and lower.

Not that he would've been worried about getting lost even if it had gotten dark before he got to the town. Not with the railroad tracks to follow. Still, he was glad to be getting there.

Snowshoe looked from this angle about like any other young mining camp. Which is to say raw and roaring.

Physically the camp was laid out like a soup bowl, the buildings of the town being in the bottom of the bowl and the mine openings and tailings dumps scattered all around the sides and rim. Most ore finds tended to be in canyon bottoms, but a good many too were found in cirques and bowls like this one. Longarm had heard geologists say that such locations were the craters of ancient volcanoes. He couldn't say that they generally looked much like his notion of what a volcano ought to be, but then he wasn't going to argue with the experts just because of that, being no experienced hand when it came to volcano recognition. The one time he'd been stony cold abso-damned-lutely certain sure positive that he was seeing a volcano was when he was young and wet behind the ears and was making his first trip into the Yellowstone country. And that, he'd been assured at the time, hadn't been volcano after all but just a geyser. Right there and then he'd determined to retire from volcano wrangling and leave that business to others who cared about the distinctions a whole lot more than Custis Long ever would.

Whichever it was then, fizzled-out volcano or the remains of a big-ass geyser, Longarm marched into this bowl where Snowshoe was located.

The lamps and lanterns were already lighted and in the windows to welcome him. Or to welcome somebody. He was willing to concede that the merchants of the town likely had workers soon to come off shift more in mind for their welcome than they did the deputy marshal who was going to piss them all off. But he would accept the lights as a nice sort of gesture anyway.

He walked past a slightly startled agent at the Bitterroot and Brightwater depot—the man no doubt was unaccustomed to seeing well-dressed gentlemen stroll in off the tracks—and on to the nearest decent-looking hotel, located predictably enough within easy reach of the railroad station.

"And how long will you be staying with us, sir?" the smiling desk clerk asked.

"Couple nights. Maybe longer. I'll let you know."

"Would you care to leave a deposit for the room then, sir?"

"No need for that," Longarm told him. He dragged out one of the voucher forms he'd gotten from Henry back in Denver and laid it down. "When I check out, friend, we'll fill this in an' I'll sign for the charges."

The clerk's smile faded and was replaced by a frown. "And what branch of government do you represent, sir?"

"Does it matter?"

"Of course not, sir. Not at all. Regardless of the branch we, um, have no vacancies at the moment."

"Now ain't that a shame," Longarm observed mildly.

"Yes, sir. Quite a pity." The clerk gave Longarm an oily, up-yours sort of look that said he was lying and didn't particularly give a shit that Longarm knew it.

"Funny how you had a room available till I laid down that voucher."

"Did I say that, sir? My error if so. Please accept my apologies."

Longarm opened his mouth to speak.

Then closed it again.

What the hell was he gonna say? Give me a room or else? Not really. This SOB hadn't done anything to be arrested for, and it probably wouldn't be a good idea for a deputy U.S. marshal to commence his visit in Snowshoe by beating up on the citizens there.

And if nothing else, this little experience gave Longarm a hint about the kind of reception he could expect in the town. Just about what he'd figured, of course, but he sure would've been willing to be proved wrong.

What it came down to, the folks there had been warned that there was a deputy on the way to spring the Utes. No surprise about that. The judge's ruling back in Nebraska would be announced to the public at the time the writ was issued. By now anybody who cared could know that the Utes of Snowshoe, Colorado, had gone and secured their release.

And given what these people undoubtedly believed about the Indians, there wasn't any other way they could've been expected to react once the knowledge reached them.

After all, members of this same Ute tribe had murdered their agent and fought a pitched battle with soldiers not so very long ago. In truth—not that it was a point Longarm would want to dwell on when he discussed the matter with any local folks—it was more than merely possible that some of the individual Utes who were there today could've participated in that fighting too. Even if by some chance there were no actual participants there in Snowshoe at the moment, it was certain that close relatives of those Utes would've been involved then.

It only stood to reason then that the white residents of Snowshoe would be reacting out of fear. They would honestly believe that the Utes in the neighborhood might up and go on the warpath anytime at all, with or without warning, with or without justification.

Never mind that these particular Ute Indians had the same rights as anybody else. Never mind that anybody, including an Indian, should be treated as innocent until guilty. Never mind, even, that there hadn't been any crimes committed yet for anybody to be guilty of.

What it came right down to was that there were Utes in the vicinity and the white settlers were scared of 'em. That was the bare-bones truth of it.

And if Custis Long wanted to come in there and set the Utes loose in that community, the townspeople would see it as him coming in there and giving a bunch of Indians permission to run wild.

Longarm understood all that.

He also understood that understanding the problem wasn't going to make him a lick more comfortable tonight when he was wanting a hot bath and a soft bed to help him over the aches and pains of getting there.

"Next time," Longarm said curtly, picking up his lodging voucher and shoving it back into a coat pocket.

Dammit anyhow.

He turned and stalked the hell out of there in search of somewhere else he might be able to secure a room and a meal.

Chapter 13

This was getting kinda serious. There were two hotels in Snowshoe and seven boardinghouses and no telling how many privately owned homes where a paying guest might be welcomed. Normally welcomed, that is. So far Longarm hadn't found any sort of place that would rent him a room.

Not that he had tried all of them exactly. But he had tried both hotels and three of the boardinghouses without success.

After the first couple of rejections he'd gotten wise that it wasn't going to help any if he flopped out a government payment voucher for his stay, and had resigned himself to paying cash out of pocket and then fighting it out with Henry and Billy Vail about reimbursement.

By then, dammit, even that hadn't been possible. By then the word was around, complete with description: That sonuvabitch marshal's in town, boys. Don't nobody lift a finger to help him. And in particular don't nobody give him a room where he can rest his weary ass.

Not that Longarm was privy to the exact language of the warnings that were circulating. But he was willing to believe it was that or something close enough that the differences didn't matter.

The point was, he was already a marked man in Snowshoe, and an unwelcome one, and he wasn't real likely to find things pleasant there now that the word was out.

He gave up looking for a room and decided to settle for the local law. There was an unwritten code that said one lawman helped another no matter what personal differences might exist between them. Longarm figured to capitalize on that now so he would have a place to sleep tonight that wouldn't involve cold breezes down the back of his neck and a mattress made of pea gravel.

"Mind telling me where I can find your county sheriff or town marshal or, uh, police chief? Whoever's in charge o' the law here?" he asked the next man he saw on the street, a nicely dressed man in sleeve garters and a crisp collar who might have been a merchant or a banker or something similar.

"That'd be Chief Bevvy," the man said.

"Bevvy?"

"Ayuh. Chief of Police Robert Bevvy. Known as Boo to his friends."

"Boo Bevvy," Longarm repeated.

"Ayuh. But if you're who I think you are, mister, you'd best call him Chief an' tug your forelock when you do."

"That sort o' thing isn't a habit o' mine," Longarm confessed.

"Excellent," the gentleman chortled. "I recommend you stand by your guns, sir. In fact, go right ahead and call our chief Boo. I could use the business."

Longarm raised an eyebrow.

"Allow me to introduce myself, sir. Dr. Heygood Capwell, physician to the community of Snowshoe. Also entrepreneur, commodities speculator, mining shares investor, raconteur, hale fellow, bodacious wit, occasional imbiber, and, um"— he grinned—"part-time mortician as well."

"It's only fair t' tell you that I don't figure to give you no business," Longarm said with a smile. "Not if I can help it, I won't."

"We shall see, Marshal. We shall see. And your name was?"

"Was an' still is Custis Long. Known as Longarm to my friends."

"Very well, Marshal Long." Capwell bowed formally. Longarm felt a momentary pang of disappointment. He'd hoped that at least this pleasant, happy-go-lucky doctor who knew who he was but smiled in spite of that would have departed from the local norm and accepted him as any other human being. But apparently that wasn't to be. Capwell was honest enough to make that clear. Longarm supposed that was something.

"You were gonna tell me where I could find Chief Bevvy, Doctor?"

"The police offices and town jail are in the basement of City Hall, Marshal Long. Two blocks down and one over. In that direction. It would be possible to miss it, I suppose, but difficult."

"Two down, one over. Thank you, Doctor."

"Good evening, Marshal."

Longarm hefted his bag and saddle—at this point he was taking the precaution of carrying the bag in his left hand and the saddle under his left arm; the arrangement wasn't comfortable but it allowed his gun hand to be free, just in case—and walked in the direction Capwell indicated, back more or less in the direction of the railroad station and the first hotel he'd stopped at.

It seemed rather fitting, he decided, that his first experience in Snowshoe was to run in circles.

The night watchman—the man was wearing a badge, but surely he was only a night watchman or jailer; a man this pigheaded and dull couldn't possibly be a town policeman—turned his head and spat a stream of thick brown juice that landed close enough to splatter the instep of Longarm's right boot.

"Closed is what I said, mister, an' closed is what I meant. Chief ain't here. Won't be till mornin'. You come back then an' ask fer the chief."

Longarm put a tight rein on his patience and forced himself to speak calm and clear. "And where can I find the chief, please?"

"Here. Tomorra. Chief Bevvy is gen'rally at his desk by eight. Never knowed him t' be later than nine. You come back here then."

Longarm thought it over. Reached a conclusion. "Very well," he said. "In the meantime I want to see the prisoners in your jail."

"When Chief Bevvy says," the watchman agreed stubbornly. "I ain't unlocking for you till."

"I've showed you my credentials," Longarm reasoned. "You know I am a deputy United States marshal. You know I have a right to see any prisoners under federal jurisdiction."

"I don't know shit 'bout that," the man said, a claim that Longarm was willing to accept at face value. "What I do know is what I tolt you a'ready. When Chief Bevvy says open 'er up, I'll open 'er up. Till then,'at door stays locked, mister. No exceptions."

"I'm not no fucking mister," Longarm barked. "I'm a deputy United States marshal."

"All right. Lemme put it this way. I'll open 'at door an' let you in when Chief Bevvy says I should. Mister Deputy United States Fucking Marshal. Sir." The SOB spat again. Closer this time.

The worst part of this was that there wasn't a damn thing Longarm could do about it short of beating the watchman up—which he could easily do—or shooting him—even easier done—and taking the jail keys from him. But what would that accomplish?

Longarm whirled and stomped away through the alley toward the public street beyond. The City Hall building, he'd found, was closed for the night and locked up. There was, however, a separate entrance in this alley. A staircase dug near the back of the alley led down to the basement-level police station and jail. That was the door that was being guarded by the dimwit with the chaw in his mouth.

Longarm hadn't been in Snowshoe more than a few hours, and already he was feeling frustrated to the point of wanting to beat the crap out of somebody. Almost anybody would've done. Just to relieve the tension.

He walked back to the front of the City Hall building, and for the lack of anything better to do set his things down on the board sidewalk there and helped himself to a seat on one of the pair of benches that flanked the doorway. It felt pretty damned good to be able to sit down, he admitted to himself. He had been on his feet practically since dawn, most of that time lugging all his traveling gear with him.

He crossed his legs and pulled out a cheroot and lighted it. The dry, tasty smoke helped to calm him down, and he was able to think clearly once he wasn't blustering and fuming in reaction to some asshole with a little authority.

Things really weren't all that bad, Longarm realized.

The townspeople might not like this, but the chief of police and any other city fathers would back off quick enough once Longarm buttonholed them and showed the actual writ to them.

Until the writ was formally served they might put on a show for the home folks. But once the service was duly and legally accomplished, they wouldn't have any choice about it but to roll over and give up.

Either that or have the full weight of the federal government come down on them.

If push came to shove, Longarm himself could summon all the assistance he required there. Up to and including the use of U.S. Army troops. Fort Union likely would be the closest, Longarm thought. Or anyway it would have the units able to get there the quickest, even if they might not be closest by a few miles. From Fort Union soldiers could cut across the passes in the south end of the Sangre de Cristos—it was easy going through there, and the Moro route started practically in the post's backyard—and that would get them clear of the worst of the mountain travel. They could cross the Rio Grande, move west to clear the southern thrust of the San Juans, and from there have an unimpeded march up the valley of the Dolores.

Longarm decided that he would by damn point all that out to the good people of Snowshoe too. Make sure they understood the seriousness of this.

Once he found someone to talk to, that is.

Dammit.

He grumped and grumbled a little more to himself, then finished his smoke and stood.

Then, for the first time in quite a while, he actually smiled.

It hadn't particularly occurred to him before now, but the City Hall building of Snowshoe was a freestanding structure built of native rock.

And there was an alley on either side of it.

That tobacco-chewing dragon might be guarding the jail entry in that alley over yonder, Longarm knew. But the alley over on this side here was another matter entire, wasn't it.

Longarm flipped the butt of his cheroot into the street and shoved his gear underneath the bench he'd just been resting on.

He tugged the tail of his coat down where it belonged, and ambled around the corner into the alley away from where that idjit watchman was.

The idea was that rooms, even basement rooms, even jail cell basement rooms, have windows.

And if Longarm couldn't officially see or have a word with the Utes he'd come here to spring loose, why, there wasn't anything would stop him from peeking in and whispering a howdy to them.

At the very least, he figured, they should know that help was on hand.

He took one last look over his shoulder, then made his way deep into the alley by feel, one hand hovering close to the butt of his Colt.

Chapter 14

Longarm was not only frustrated, he was angry. Damned angry.

City Hall was closed, the jail was closed, the police chief couldn't be located—wouldn't be was more the truth of that—and nothing, absolutely nothing was going right.

Longarm stormed into the first establishment he came to that was open for business.

"You!" He stood at the bar with an accusing finger pointing into the startled face of the nearer of the two bartenders.

"S-s-sir?"

"I'm looking for a man who lives in this shitty town. Able. Ab Able. Where do I find him? And you'd best tell me right now, by damn, or so help me . . ." He didn't bother finishing the threat. But then he didn't have to. Fury in Custis Long's eyes had been known to turn roaring bullies into meekly cooperative citizens. A slightly built, inoffensive fellow like this barkeep was not apt to cross the deputy at a moment like this.

"T-t-t-t—"

"It's all right, Henny," the other barman said quickly. "You go an' draw a short one for Mr. Babcock, please."

Henny bobbed his head frantically, never once taking his eyes off Longarm's, and fled toward the far end of the bar.

"It ain't nothing personal, mister. Henny stutters when he gets excited. He was prob'ly scared you'd think he was funning you an' smack him one." This man gave Longarm a hostile expression along with the explanation.

"Sorry," Longarm said. "I did come on a mite strong, didn't I?"

"A mite strong? Yeah, that'd be one way to put it."

"Sorry," he repeated, mostly meaning it. He was still pissed with the people of this town, but that didn't mean he wanted to go around terrorizing people like Henny.

"What was it you wanted, Marshal?" There was no pretense of not knowing who Longarm was. But then by now everyone in Snowshoe seemed to know that.

"Ab Able," he said.

The bartender frowned as if not understanding. "Ab?"

"Lawyer Able," Longarm said.

This time the barman seemed amused. "That explains it. We got a lawyer named Able. But it ain't Ab. It's A. B. Goes by the initials, like. That's what confused me since I never heard of nobody named Ab Able around here."

"All right, dammit, A. B. Able then. It makes no never mind to me. Where can I find him?"

"At this hour?"

"At this hour, dammit." Longarm was getting pissed again.

"Don't bust a gusset over it. Jeez. I can show you how to go. Whether you'd be welcome there at this hour is up to Lawyer Able, though."

"Fine," Longarm snapped. "Now give me the directions and be quick about it if you please."

The barkeep grunted and left his station to walk outside so he could point and gesture while he gave his directions.

"Thank you," Longarm said curtly when all that was said and done.

The barman didn't answer with so much as a grunt or a growl. He simply turned and went back inside.

That bartender had been right about one thing, Longarm conceded once he was standing in front of the split-log cabin where A. B. Able lived and conducted business.

66

The hour was past any reasonable time for calling on a stranger. Longarm's Ingersoll showed it to be past ten. Hardly business hours.

On the other hand, this wasn't any reasonable bit of business, Longarm decided, so the hell with it. There were things he had to know and the sooner the better. If A. B. Able objected to that, well, fuck 'im.

Longarm marched to the door of the cabin and lightly rapped on it. There wasn't any light showing inside, and the place remained dark and silent now. Longarm began to get angry again. That bartender had said Able lived there as well as having his office there. So where the hell was he? Off getting drunk someplace while his clients languished? Laying up with whores while the Utes suffered? That sort of conduct was about what Longarm would expect from anybody in Snowshoe, Colorado. Even from the lawyer who was supposed to be on the high side of things there.

The more he thought about that the madder he got. And if some polite knocking on the door didn't produce any result, maybe what he needed was a more vigorous summons.

He reared back and began bashing on the damned door. Not trying to knock it down exactly. But not much interested in being gentle with it either.

He finished off by giving the sonuvabitch door a couple of kicks just for good measure.

That didn't make him feel much better, but he'd damned well wanted to do it and so he had.

Now, he supposed, he could turn around and go look for a place where he could spread his blanket for the damned night. What was left of it. He quit pounding on the lawyer's door.

"I . . . have a gun," a quavering, timorous female voice called softly from inside the cabin. "G-go away or I'll shoot. I will."

Just that quick Longarm went from feeling pissed to feeling like nine kinds of an idiot.

Nobody'd told him that Lawyer Able had a wife, for God's sake.

Not that he'd asked.

But even so . . .

"Ma'am? Mrs. Able? Lordy, ma'am, I do apologize. I've woke you up and scared you and . . . well, I don't know what all else I've gone and done. Made a fool of myself, that's for sure. This is Custis Long, Mrs. Able. Can you hear me? My name is Custis Long. Deputy U.S. Marshal Long, ma'am. I've come here to see Mr. Able about those Ute Indians, ma'am. Could you . . . if it wouldn't be too much trouble, ma'am, after I've gone and bothered you like this, could you please tell me where I might find Mr. Able? Please?"

"You say your name is Long?" He was pleased to note that the lady's voice sounded better now, more in control of herself. At least she didn't sound like she was in immediate fear for her life this time.

"Yes, ma'am, it is."

"Would you mind verifying that, please?"

"Glad to, ma'am. I have my credentials right here."

"Would you do it without me having to open my door, please?"

"Ma'am, I don't know how I'd manage that."

"What do the Indians call you, Marshal?"

"They call me Long Arm, Miz Able. Longarm is my regular nickname."

"Wait there a moment. I'll open up."

"Yes, ma'am. Thank you."

He could hear movement inside, then the sounds of bolts being drawn. At least two steel bolts on the inside of the door here, he thought, plus a wooden bar. And wasn't that almighty strange. Generally speaking, a lady was safe from harm in these mining camps. Man-made kinds of harm anyway. She might work herself to death or come down with disease. Even starve. But it was a rare—and stupid— son of a bitch of a man who'd ever lay an unwelcome finger on a woman in any Western town Longarm'd ever known. Any man who'd do a thing like that wouldn't live long enough to be strung up by a mob. He'd be torn to pieces before he could be dragged to a tree for the hanging. Decent men simply didn't put up with that kind of shit in this country. So why in hell was Mrs. Able so frightened?

Just a timid sort maybe, Longarm thought. Some folks were like that whether they needed to be or not.

He heard the bolts being pulled and the bar lifted aside. Then the door came open a fraction of an inch and he could see the shine of moonlight striking an eye that was applied to the miniscule opening. The woman was inspecting him before she allowed the door to open any farther.

"You really are Longarm?" One positive sign was that her voice seemed calm and rational now. That was good.

"Yes, ma'am." He pulled out his wallet and opened it so she could see the badge that was pinned there. There wasn't light enough for her to examine it thoroughly, but there wasn't much he could do about that.

"Give me a moment, Marshal. I'll find my robe and light a lamp. Then you can come in."

"If you'd just tell me where I can find Mr. Able, ma'am."

"Please wait where you are, Marshal," she said crisply. Before Longarm could say any more the door was pushed fully closed—but not bolted again while he was standing there at it, he noticed. Nice to know that he wasn't the one she was scared of. He could hear the faint sounds of someone moving inside.

He shrugged and resigned himself to doing this however Mrs. Able wanted. Not that he had much choice about it. He didn't know where else to look for A. B. Able.

And anyway, this reception, bad as it might otherwise seem, was nevertheless the warmest and most welcoming he'd yet had in Snowshoe. Hell, he probably ought to savor and enjoy it while he had the chance because from here on in things were likely to go downhill.

Chapter 15

When next the cabin door opened, Longarm might have thought he was in a completely different place from where he'd been just a few minutes earlier.

Instead of being scared and nervous, Mrs. Able was gracious and charming in her welcome. She'd taken time to light several lamps inside, and was carrying another. Moreover, she looked mighty nice too.

Longarm had no idea how she'd been dressed or what she'd looked like when he'd dragged her out of a sound sleep to come to the door, but now she looked elegant and lovely in a velvet dressing gown that had frilly wisps of ruffle showing daintily at throat and wrists.

Her hair had been loosened for sleeping, of course, and Longarm certainly did not mind it hanging thick and free like it was. Her hair was a dark rich red in color, which contrasted quite fetchingly with the deep blue of the dressing gown.

Her complexion was that creamy perfection that redheads are always supposed to have but seldom do.

Longarm judged that Mrs. Able was in her early thirties or thereabouts. And decidedly attractive. Lawyer Able was one helluva lucky man in his opinion.

"I apologize again for waking you, ma'am. It's just that I considered it important."

"Please come in, Marshal." She showed him to an upholstered armchair next to a lamp and table. The cabin was divided into two rooms of roughly equal size. Longarm had no idea what was in the other, but the front room was

70

furnished as an office with a desk, storage cabinets, and several chairs arranged for conversation and reading. There was a sheet-metal heating stove at one end, but no sign of a cooking range or any sort of kitchenware. He guessed that the bedroom area must also double as the kitchen. Either that or the back part of the cabin had been cut into several tiny rooms instead of one room of serviceable size.

"A drink, Marshal?" She was standing close by, ready to provide the refreshment if he wished.

"No, thank you, ma'am. If you would just direct me to—"

"That shallow dish beside you is used as an ashtray if you care to smoke, Marshal. I don't mind."

"Yes, ma'am, thank you. Now if you'd just—"

"I believe you have a writ in your possession signed by Judge McFee?"

"Yes, ma'am, but—"

The lady cut him off once again, but this time she sighed and turned away. She went to the rolltop desk that was the dominant piece of furniture in the small room, sat down there, and swiveled the chair to face him.

"You are determined to keep it up, aren't you?" she asked.

"Ma'am?"

"Oh, never mind. It isn't your fault. I daresay it isn't even my fault. It is no one's. And everyone's." The lady looked sad now.

"Ma'am?" he repeated, feeling more confused than ever.

"As I say, Marshal, the fault is not yours. The misconceptions are just so . . . infuriatingly common. Something I must face over and over again every day of my life. Sometimes I tire of it, that's all."

"I'm sorry, Mrs. Able, but I don't know what you're talking about." Longarm decided to take the lady up on that offer to smoke in her presence. He pulled out a cheroot, nipped off the twist, and rolled the tasty leaf on his tongue. There was a jar of broom straws provided on the table, so he didn't have to waste a match to light his smoke. He lit a

71

straw in the lamp flame and used that to light the cheroot.

"My point exactly, Marshal," the woman said.

"I hate t' repeat myself, ma'am. But what *are* you talkin' about?"

"I am not Mrs. Able, Marshal."

"No?"

"There is no Mrs. Able."

"Ma'am, really now, I didn't come here t' pry into any private, uh, situations. Between you an' Mr. Able, that is. Or, um, anybody else."

"I'm not making myself clear, am I?"

"No, ma'am, I would have to say that you are not," he agreed.

"Marshal Long, the point I am trying to make here is that there is no *Mister* Able either," the lady said. As if that was supposed to explain everything. Longarm would've been satisfied if it had just explained *some*thing.

"Are you tryin' t' tell me, ma'am, that Judge McFee back in Nebraska has issued a writ o' habeas corpus on behalf of a lawyer that don't exist?" He whistled and shook his head. "Lordy, ma'am, I don't know how that one is gonna set when they find out about it."

"Marshal. Longarm. May I call you Longarm?"

He nodded.

"You still misunderstand. There is an attorney named Able. A. B. Able. Agnes Bertha Able."

"Is that what you been hemming and hawing about, ma'am? Good grief, you been wasting my time for nothing. What I wanta know, Miss Able, is where the hell the Utes are that I'm supposed to serve papers for? I just been over to the jail, and it's empty 'cept for a couple drunks. Now would you please quit fretting about gender and get down to some business with me here?"

Chapter 16

Once she got over the shock of realizing that Custis Long honestly didn't give a shit if she was male, female, or something else entirely, just so she was the lawyer he'd come there to see, she was brisk, bright, and informative.

"The Indians in question," she said, "are being held in an old mine shaft close to town. The jail wasn't large enough, and I agreed that it wasn't healthy for the women or the children to be caged in public view like that. The quarters at the mine are not really very good, but they are better than the jail would have been. The Indians agreed to the arrangement, and as their attorney of record I concurred, Longarm."

"That takes a load off my mind. I was wondering if the police chief was up to something."

"I'm sure Boo will release the prisoners once service of the writ is made, Longarm. I can't imagine him doing otherwise."

"Could get it done tonight, I reckon, if you know where he lives."

"Frankly I would rather do it in daylight. You won't believe the levels of fear and animosity that exist in this town."

"I think I might," he commented, but didn't push the point any further than that.

"It frightens even me, Longarm. I've had bolts installed on my door. Six months ago I wouldn't have believed that necessary, yet it is true. And when we do secure the release of those people from custody, I want it to be in broad daylight so we can see if there is anyone lurking about with guns."

"That bad, huh?"

"That bad," she said.

"I'll accept your judgment on it," he said. "We won't try and do anything until tomorrow."

"Thank you." She stood. "Would you care for a drink now, Longarm?"

"You wouldn't have any rye, would you?"

"Sorry. Calvados is the best I can do."

"Ma'am?"

She smiled. "Applejack, Longarm. Hard cider that's gone down and dirty. It will put hair on your chest, guaranteed."

"Reckon I'd best try some then."

"Good. I hope you won't mind if I join you?"

"Good likker is always better in good company," he said.

One of the cabinets that he had assumed held files instead held a black glass bottle in an odd, bulbous shape. Aggie Able poured generous measures into a pair of water glasses and gave one to Longarm. This time she chose to sit in the comfortable chair across the lamp table from his rather than returning to her desk.

"To your good health," she said by way of a toast.

"Hair on your chest," he agreed, and Aggie laughed.

The lady downed half of hers at a gulp. Longarm followed her example. And had to gasp for breath. "Lordy," he blurted out when he was able to talk again. "That stuff is stout. I never knew you could put fire in a jug like that." He grinned. "Good, though."

"I'm glad you like it." Aggie set her glass down and opened a small wooden box that was sitting next to the lamp. Longarm had thought it an overlarge matchbox. Actually it contained some thin, cheap, sweet-leaf cheroots. He recognized the type. Molasses-soaked wrapper leafs and rum-soaked fillers in a vain attempt to smooth out the flavors of a basically worthless tobacco. Floor sweepings,

74

Longarm figured. They cost a tenth what his own fine brand went for. And at that the things were viciously overpriced.

"You aren't gonna smoke one of them things, are you?" he asked when Aggie took one out.

"Do I shock you?"

"Hell, no, but you disappoint me, not having any better taste than thàt. Here." He got out one of his own cheroots and passed it to her. Aggie smelled of it, then sniffed at her own. She raised an eyebrow.

"If you're gonna do it," he suggested, "at least learn t' do it with style."

She laughed and accepted a light from him, cupping her hands over his and guiding the flaming straw to her thin cigar. Longarm wasn't sure, but he thought there just might be more heat in the touch of her hands on his than there was in that burning straw tip. She sat there with a cheroot in one hand and a glass of fiery brandy in the other and gave him a lingering look of intense speculation. Speculation? he wondered then. Or promise?

He suspected, though, that Aggie Able wasn't half as down-deep genuine tough as she wanted to make herself out to be. He kept remembering how timid she'd been when he was pounding on her door in the dark. That image was quite a contrast with this one.

Not that either one was his to worry about. Lawyer Able, quirky though she might be, was welcome to be and to do just as she pleased. She didn't need his permission for any of it.

"When did you get in?" she asked, obviously wanting to strike up a conversation while they drank and smoked together.

He told her, and added a few bits about the lack of cooperation he'd found among her fellow townspeople. He played the tales for laughs, though; he wasn't much on complaint.

"It could have been worse," she said.

"Uh, huh. As it is, no harm done."

"Thank goodness."

"How d'you get along here? I mean, you bein' a lady lawyer an' representing the Utes too?"

"Gracious, Longarm, I was already such a pariah that this thing with the Indians hardly added anything. Most of the men in town, certainly all the leading gentlemen of the community, were already convinced that I'm lesbian. Or worse. But I get along. The wives of those same men like me, you see. I'm something of a role model for them. Not that they want to become like me, exactly, but it pleases them to see that a woman can be free and independent if she wishes. So I get by." She laughed and added, "It helps quite a lot, of course, that I'm rich."

Longarm couldn't help but chuckle. And then, involuntarily, he looked around at the small cabin where Aggie lived.

"Comfortable," the lady corrected herself, obviously guessing what he'd been thinking. "Not dependent on them for my livelihood, anyway."

"I can see how that'd help."

Aggie tossed back the rest of her drink and went to fetch the bottle. She poured seconds for both of them and resumed her seat. "I've never known a deputy marshal before," she said out of nowhere. "Are they all like you?"

He shrugged. "Mostly, I suppose. More or less."

"You don't mind that I'm a lawyer and a woman."

"Nope."

"I'm a good lawyer, Longarm."

He nodded agreeably and took a sip of the applejack. The more he had of the stuff the smoother and tastier it got.

"I'm a good woman too."

He nodded again.

"Do you have hair on your chest?"

"Bound to have. You guaranteed that I would, remember?"

"What if I want to see for myself?"

"Reckon I wouldn't wrestle you t' prevent it."

"You know, of course, that you won't find any place to sleep in Snowshoe tonight. But I could put you up here. I only have one bed."

He sipped the calvados again. It was really right nice.

"A woman in my position wouldn't dare let her defenses down, Longarm. Not with any of the men here no matter how attractive they might be."

"No, I can see where that'd be a bad idea."

"It wouldn't do me any good with the ladies either if I started sleeping around with the men here. I wouldn't be an inspiration to them any longer but a threat. They would worry that I might take their husbands away. Better if they think I'm sexless. Or lesbian. Can you believe it? I've never been openly propositioned by a man in this town, but two of the women have tried to seduce me. And they weren't ladies of the night who did that either. Both of them were respectable married women."

"I'd believe it," Longarm said.

"I am not carved from stone, Longarm. I have feelings just like anyone. I have needs. I haven't felt a man's arms around me since I came here. Not once, Longarm."

He set his drink down on the table, and carefully stubbed his cheroot out in the ashtray.

"Does that stuff put hair on a lady's chest too?" he asked.

"We shall have to look and see," Aggie suggested.

He stood, took her by the hand, and pulled her to her feet. He disposed of her glass and her cigar, then bent and slipped one arm behind her knees, the other behind her back. He lifted her off her feet, cradling her across his chest. Agnes Bertha Able was a much more substantial female than he'd expected. Not enough to buckle his knees or anything close to it, but certainly more than he'd bargained for. Still, he managed to make her think she was feather light and that he could carry her like this indefinitely if he wished. This, he figured, this sort of domination by a man, a possession of sorts, was very likely what she really needed more than anything else.

77

He could feel that already her breath was coming in short, panting gasps. No priming needed, she was already set to explode. By now he bet her drawers were already soaked. She put her arms around him and buried her face against the side of his neck while he carried her into the bedroom, leaving the office lights burning to be tended afterward if anyone wanted to bother.

Chapter 17

"That was wonderful, Longarm. Marvelous. I haven't felt this good in . . . I can't tell you when. Never, I suppose. Not like this. Not ever this good before." She reached down and gave his cock a squeeze.

A slightly too vigorous squeeze, actually. He winced and tried not to show the pain.

Aggie fetched an ashtray from the bedside and balanced it on her chest. Longarm took the hint and lighted cheroots for both of them.

"I think I forgot to tell you earlier, but these cigars of yours are wonderful. Much better than those awful things I've been buying. I never would have believed there could be so much difference."

"Quality," he said. "It counts in everything."

"So it does," she agreed. "So it does." She smiled. "And now I know what quality in a man is too." This time he was able to intercept her hand before she got to him. If she missed the cock and grabbed his nuts by mistake she might turn them into pulp. He squeezed her hand, smiled, raised it to his lips, and kissed her knuckles one by one. She liked that well enough that he could see her turning wet and horny all over again. "You are a beautiful man, Custis Long. Marvelous. Has anyone ever told you before that you are beautiful? It doesn't embarrass you, does it?"

"It doesn't embarrass me," he said.

"Has anyone ever told you before that you are beautiful?"

"No," he lied. "Never."

"You're beautiful." She turned her head and kissed his chest.

What she was looking for, of course, was some compliments coming back her way. And shit, he supposed there wouldn't be any getting around it. She'd just keep fishing until she caught something. He might as well do it now and get it done with.

But not the truth. Lordy, Lordy, not the truth, the whole truth, nothing but the truth. Shee-it, not that.

Longarm smiled and leaned close so he could look the woman square in the eyes.

"You're pretty wonderful yourself," he said, and kissed her.

The flavor of her kisses was nice. Smoke and applejack and horny female all blended together. That was a combination that made for a tasty stew.

And Aggie had herself one helluva nice body. Full and lush and a tad on the plump side. But creamy. Oh, my, soft and creamy.

Proud tits as big as pumpkins. Bright red nipples. Soft mound of belly. Big creamy thighs. Bright pink pussy winking through a veil of copper-colored pubic hair. Aggie had it all.

The only thing wrong was that the poor woman didn't know what the hell to do with it.

It was just plain damned lucky for her that she found it so easy to reach a climax. Most women couldn't, not without some patience and a knowledgeable man applying himself to the job of making them scream and go wild. Some women never came, not in their whole lives.

Not Aggie, though. Pinch her nipple and she'd shudder. Touch her clitoris and she'd go into convulsions. Shove a cock—hell, a finger, a toe, probably a banana or any other damned thing—into her cunt and she'd turn herself inside out and shriek loud enough to rattle the shingles on the roof.

Aggie was what a man might think of as being easy to please.

Which was fine, of course. Longarm thought every woman ought to have it so good.

Except Aggie never had learned to keep up her end of the deal.

Once he got in the saddle a guy was on his own as far as Aggie was concerned. By then she'd had her explosion and was waiting for the next impulses to build. Whatever the guy wanted to do to amuse himself in the meantime was okay by her. But she wasn't going to participate in it.

She just lay there.

A guy could get as much response out of a bowl of warm oatmeal as he could out of Aggie once she'd come.

Come to think of it, Longarm decided, the oatmeal might be the better fuck. Tighter. He had no idea what might've happened to stretch her cunt out, but he suspected it was big enough that she didn't need a handbag. She could just shove stuff into her snatch instead.

All in all, the woman was a disappointment of the first water.

"You're beautiful," he said. "Lovely."

"Was it good for you, Longarm?"

"Wonderful."

"It was for me too." She tried to reach for his cock, but he kept a tight grip on her hand.

"Tell me, Aggie, do you enjoy French style?"

"I don't understand."

He explained it to her.

"Longarm! You can't be serious. In my mouth? But you pee with that. And you want me to put it into my mouth? Ick. How disgusting."

"It was only a thought."

"Well, think again. That's awful."

"Sorry." He reached between those magnificent tits and deposited some cigar ash onto the china dish she'd set on her chest.

Helluva body, he thought.

Helluva waste.

"I'm getting sleepy, pretty lady. How 'bout you?"

"One more time first. Please?"

He forced a smile. "I was hoping that's what you'd say."

Chapter 18

The community's tolerance for their eccentric lady lawyer did not extend to the federal deputy she'd caused to be there. If Aggie hadn't been with him, Longarm doubted he could have gotten the clerk at City Hall to look in his direction. Although even at that, her presence was a mixed blessing. Aggie Able in private seemed quite a different woman from Agnes Able in public.

"John."

"Yes, Miss Agnes?"

"Answer the deputy's question, John."

"Sorry, ma'am. I didn't hear him ask one."

"John. Really now."

"But I didn't. Honest."

"Well, we aren't going to argue about it, are we. Now, please. Answer the gentleman's question, John, and quickly, quickly."

The clerk, John, gave Longarm a pointedly vacant look, but waited without comment for Longarm to repeat a question he'd already asked three times without response.

"Where is the police chief this morning, mister?" Longarm asked.

"If he isn't downstairs, then I wouldn't know," John said. It was a barefaced lie, as was plain in his tone of voice and his smug, smirking demeanor. And there was shit-for-all that Longarm could do about it.

"John!" Aggie chided.

"Sorry, Miss Agnes. I don't happen to know, that's all."

"You know, of course, it won't do any good for the police chief or the mayor or whoever else to hide from me," Longarm said. "I'll serve my writ on whoever is guarding those Indians, and they will be released on the spot."

"I wouldn't know about any of that," John insisted. "You asked me a question, I gave you an answer. Is there anything else you want?"

"No, I suppose not," Longarm said, conceding an impasse if not exactly a defeat.

The clerk nodded smugly and went back to whatever it was he did on behalf of the good citizens of Snowshoe.

"Well?" Aggie asked.

"Let's go get those people out of custody," Longarm said.

"Shouldn't we have breakfast first?"

He thought that sounded like a damned strange question coming from the Indians' own lawyer. He would've expected her to be even more eager to get the paper served than he was. Apparently that wasn't quite so.

Not that he wasn't hungry at the moment. It seemed that Lawyer Able had many talents—he was sure that she must, otherwise she never would have made it into the practice of law—but cooking was no more her forte than screwing was. At least she was aware that she couldn't cook, and therefore didn't bother trying.

"We'll have breakfast later," Longarm insisted.

"A cup of coffee on our way?"

"Later."

"You needn't snap at me like that. After all, dear, it is your own fault that I'm so famished this morning."

"Quit batting your eyelashes at me, Aggie. You ain't the type for it."

She sulked up into a pout, but the expression lasted only for a moment. Then she laughed and took his elbow. "All right, Longarm. I give up. We shall tend to business first and have our pleasures afterward."

"Fine." He hoped—but of course couldn't say—that Aggie's notions about pleasures after duty weren't going to extend to any more sweaty two-party masturbations on that bed of hers. Which was about the way he viewed having to hump the woman. It was no better, and in some ways not so much fun, as screwing Five Finger Mamie.

"This way," she said crisply.

Aggie led him not directly to the mine where the Utes were being kept, but to a ramshackle livery barn on the edge of town. "I don't own a carriage," she explained, "but I pay a retainer fee for first call against the rigs Marty has here."

At the livery she acted for all the world like she owned the place. For that matter, maybe she did. She ordered the employees around like they were her own personal servants, and was imperiously precise about which rig she wanted, which horse in the traces, even which set of harness was to be fitted and which whip placed in the socket. Longarm saw that he wouldn't want to work for this woman. If he'd been Marty or Bill at the livery, he knew he would've refused Aggie's business rather than put up with her shit. It was just as well, then, that he wasn't either one of them, he supposed.

He made a point to thank both men for their help once the rig was delivered and Aggie was aboard it. The outfit she'd selected was a light two-wheeled cart drawn by a high-stepping gray gelding in fancy harness. There was even a purple plume set atop the headstall, for cryin' out loud. Longarm felt almost embarrassed to get onto the seat beside Aggie in a turnout so silly.

He felt doubly so because she had quite automatically helped herself to the driving side of the seat and had the reins and whip in hand.

Fortunately, nothing lasts forever. Including embarrassment.

Longarm crawled onto the seat beside her and reached for a cheroot. He winked at the men who worked at the livery, and propped a boot onto the gracefully curved splashboard in front of him. "Wake me when we get there," he said, and tipped his Stetson down over his eyes.

Chapter 19

"I don't understand," Agnes Able whispered. She sounded, and looked, completely befuddled. "I can't . . . I can't believe this, Longarm."

He grunted and jumped down off the cart.

The truth was that he wasn't half so amazed as Miss Able. Although he would have had to admit to being at least a little bit surprised. After all, not many community leaders were as dumb as these folks in Snowshoe seemed to be.

Longarm stalked across an expanse of flat gravel to the gate and looked inside, even though that was done mostly for the sake of formality. The gate was standing open, and it was plenty obvious that there wasn't anybody around. Not guards and not prisoners either.

This mine and the newly erected stockade around its shaft opening were empty. Empty and vacant and no sign whatsoever of the Ute Indians who'd been held there.

"They were here . . . I guess it was the day before yesterday would have been the last time I saw them," Aggie said. She too had climbed down from the cart, and came to stand beside him. She kept staring with disbelief inside the empty stockade and shaking her head from side to side. "I drove up and talked with Bray Swind and some of the other Indians. That was after I'd received the telegram saying my writ was granted and that you would be coming to serve it. The people

86

were all so happy. They were anxious to get back into the mountains. Now . . . this. I just can't believe it, Longarm. I truly can't."

"An' I can't blame you for that neither. Stupid bastards to try an' pull something like this. How long d' they figure they can hide out from the Ewe Ess gov'ment?"

"I thought Boo had more sense than this, Longarm. I truly did."

"I believe you, Counselor." He pulled out a cheroot and lighted it without remembering to offer one to Aggie. But then it simply wasn't normal or proper for a man to have to remember to offer a cigar to a lady. "You don't s'pose . . . ," he ventured, then shook his head and allowed the sentence to die uncompleted.

"What is that, Longarm?"

"Nothing," he said. "Look, why don't you wait here a minute. I'm gonna take a look inside that mine before we start back down."

"What's the matter, Longarm? Never saw inside a mine shaft before?" she asked in a teasing tone. Then she saw the seriousness in his eyes and guessed the reason why he wanted to look inside. One hand flew to her throat, and she gasped. "No. You can't think . . . no." She shook her head quite firmly. "They may be foolish, Longarm, but they are not maniacal. They wouldn't have done anything like . . . that . . . to innocent people. Not that."

Longarm grimaced and turned away to spit. "Nobody'd slaughter innocent folks," he agreed. "But you gotta remember, Aggie, that these idjits are thinking of your Ute clients as savages an' murderers. Not as innocent folks who happen t' be Injins. So I reckon I'll take a look inside there 'fore we start back again."

The lady lawyer looked like she might burst into tears at any moment. She spun away from Longarm and went stumbling back toward the waiting cart.

Longarm ambled forward. The upper levels of this mine were obviously abandoned and empty now, and he felt no threat of danger here. His only fear was that somewhere inside the earth there was a newly made mass grave and a supply of helpless Utes to fill it.

If the town fathers of Snowshoe turned out to've been that incredibly stupid . . .

Chapter 20

"Well?"

Longarm shook his head. "Nothing." But he didn't consider the hour he'd just spent underground as time wasted.

"Thank goodness," Aggie said. The relief was plain in her expression. She too must have been having thoughts about where the Utes might have disappeared to. And bodies were all too easily disposed of in abandoned mine shafts.

Longarm lighted a smoke for himself, this time remembered to give her one too—he was soon going to have to replenish his supply if this kept up—and pulled his tweed coat back on. It hadn't been warm down in the mine, not hardly, but it had been stuffy. He'd felt better without the coat.

"Where would you suggest we look for your clients next, Counselor?" he asked.

Lawyer Able frowned and nibbled at her lower lip while she thought about the question. "I don't know," she said after taking what seemed a rather long time to come up with so unimaginative a response.

"No idea?" he prodded.

"There are so many places they could be, you see. Old prospect holes. Isolated cabins. There are even natural cave formations in this part of the country. Ancient ruins too if you believe some of the stories. I really wouldn't have any idea where Boo might have taken them."

Longarm grunted.

"We have to find them, Longarm. Those Indians haven't done anything criminal. They are entitled to their freedom. No matter what Boo and his silly male friends may think."

Longarm grunted. He wasn't in any position to argue with her. Hell, what she said was exactly what he'd come there to enforce.

Of course Billy Vail hadn't entirely had it in mind that the subjects of the writ in Custis Long's pocket would disappear once he got there.

"Do you believe that, Counselor, or are you only wanting to rub those male friends' noses in something of your doing?"

Aggie stiffened, her shoulders drawing back and her nose hiking skyward. "That is a disgusting thing for you to say, Deputy."

"It was just curiosity. Nothing personal." He'd begun to suspect, though, that Lawyer Able was much less interested in the welfare of her clients than she might have been. Otherwise how could she have lost them in the first place? And once they were lost, how could she not be ranting and raving and demanding a confrontation with the police chief and town fathers down in Snowshoe? As it was, fancy sentiments notwithstanding, she seemed content to sit there in the sunshine like they were on a picnic instead of a mission of justice.

"I do not appreciate that sort of curiosity, Deputy."

"I'm sorry," he lied.

She sniffed. "Very well then. Shall we start down now?"

"In a minute." He took a slow loop around the crudely constructed stockade, which he guessed had been recently built for the purpose of containing the Utes, as there wasn't any reason to put such a rig around a mine.

"What are you doing?"

"Looking for sign. See if I can track along behind them."

"Really? Can I watch?" She sounded interested in that, and came bouncing over to join him. Unfortunately, there wasn't anything for her to see.

90

"This is lousy country to try an' track in," he explained. "It's all either rock or gravel, an' neither one o' them will take a print. Besides, what with all the wagons that rolled in an' outta here when the mine was operating, there just ain't any way to tell what's new and what's old. Assuming the people were moved by wagon, that is. If they walked away I'd never be able to find sign of it, not on ground this hard. Not unless one o' them was leaving a deliberate trail to show where they'd gone." He sighed. "But I wanted t' be sure there wasn't nothing to see before we start back down."

"We'll go back now, Longarm, and have lunch. Then we can find Boo or the mayor and get this all cleared up."

"Huh, uh."

"Pardon me?"

"What we'll do, Counselor, is go down an' find the police chief or the mayor or whoever an' get this business cleared up. Then we'll think 'bout lunch."

She gave him a pouting look, which he ignored. "Come along, Aggie."

He helped her onto the driving box of the cart, then climbed up beside her. She wheeled the gray back in the direction from which they'd just come and set it into a slow lope, its fancy purple plume bobbing with all the monotonous regularity of a metronome. Longarm folded his arms and closed his eyes, trying to catch up on a little more of the rest he'd missed out on the night before.

One good thing, he reflected. Nobody in the vicinity seemed angry enough to start shooting at him.

Of course the locals were having things go all their own way about this so far. Or so they believed. Longarm knew better than to count on things staying peaceable once he commenced getting his licks in. So it likely was a good idea to rest up all he could now. Might not be opportunity for dozing in the sunshine much longer.

Chapter 21

The City Hall clerk named John looked up with a start when Longarm came bursting in, Counselor Able at his heels. The man actually stood and took half a step toward a side door before he got control of himself and determined to brazen it out. "Yes, Marshal?"

"Where?" Longarm demanded.

"Where's what?"

"The police chief," Longarm said.

"But I already told you—"

"The mayor," Longarm snapped. He'd reached John's desk by then, and swept around it so that he was staring the clerk eyeball to eyeball. The difference was that Longarm's eyeballs were set a good five inches higher off the floor than John's were. John commenced to look uncomfortable.

"I . . . don't know."

"Bullshit."

"I don't. I swear I don't."

"Justice of the peace."

John shook his head. "I don't know, Marshal."

"Town councilmen."

John's lips firmed into a thin line and he began to look smug instead of worried. Aggie stood beside Longarm although her presence wasn't so intimidating as his. The lady lawyer might be tolerated by the men of this town, but she was only liked by the women. John obviously wasn't much concerned about anything Aggie might threaten.

92

"Got any other elected officials here?" Longarm asked.

John, feeling much better with the situation now, gave Longarm a shit-eating grin and a loud, derisive snort. "Nope, that about covers the subject."

"How 'bout appointed officers o' the town or the country?" Longarm asked.

"Nope. Just them that you mentioned already. And I don't know where none of 'em is right now, Marshal." The lie sparkled in his eyes, and he had to struggle to keep a straight face while he was telling it.

Longarm took a step backward and gave the clerk a long looking over. The man continued to look smug.

"I say you're lying."

"Your opinion," was all John would concede.

"Lying is one thing, mister. Obstructing justice is another. I say you're obstructing justice. Now d'you want to tell me where I can find them folks? Or d'you want to sit in a jail cell while you think it over?"

"You can't do that. Hell, it's only your word against mine." John glanced at Aggie for the first time. "Tell him, Miss Agnes."

"I'm sorry, John, but a deputy United States marshal has a duty to arrest you if he believes you are obstructing an investigation. You will have the right to argue your case before a judge, of course. And to apply for bonded release or a writ of habeas corpus. Just like any other citizen." She hesitated only a fraction of a second, then couldn't help adding, "Any citizen, John. White or red."

"But I haven't—"

"Tell me what I want to know or tell your problems to a judge," Longarm said coldly.

"Judge Wilkins is out of town," John complained. "No one knows when he'll be back."

"Wouldn't matter nohow," Longarm assured him. "D'you insist on going crossways with me, bub, it's a federal court you'll come before, not some local yahoo. Think about that a minute, John. Then you work it out what you want t' do."

John's eyes squeezed shut. The expression seemed one of fear and frustration rather than thought.

And Longarm was quite frankly amazed.

The clerk's decision had been reached even before Longarm's questions were posed.

"I don't know where none of them fellows are, Marshal. You can do whatever you want, but I won't say a word different from that. I don't know and I can't tell you."

"You are a poor liar," Longarm accused.

"You can't prove that."

"You surprise me, John. You really do."

John stiffened but didn't say a damn thing.

Longarm turned him around and slapped handcuffs on his wrists. Even with steel on him, though, the man didn't relent. He'd gotten his orders, obviously, and he was carrying through with what he'd been told.

It took a powerful persuasion to do that, Longarm knew.

More powerful than a simple thing like the release of some Ute Indians should justify, dammit.

"D'you think you're protecting this community from a massacre, John? Is that it?"

The clerk didn't answer.

"What if I tell you that I'll take the Utes away from here just as quick as I get them released from custody. I'm pretty sure I can arrange that. They know me. They trust me enough, I think, to move if I ask them to. After all, it's time they start down for the spring hunt anyhow. Once they're released, mister, they're gone." Popular notion, Longarm knew, had it that the mountains in winter were a death trap of snow and ice and were to be avoided. In truth, as the Indians had known for more generations than a man could count, the mountains offered comfort and shelter in winter. Contrary to ordinary belief, the Indians moved to the plains to hunt during the warm months, but spent their winters in the high country. Their regular seasonal movements, therefore, would be taking them away from Snowshoe except for the delays imposed on them by people here. "Now does that make any difference, mister? Tell me where I can find the elected officials o' this town . . . or just tell me where I can find those Utes . . . and I'll let you go, won't file charges against you."

The man didn't so much as take time to consider it. "You go t' hell, Marshal."

"Longarm," Aggie said. "You aren't really going to—"

"Watch me," he growled. He took hold of John's elbow and guided the clerk toward the stairwell that led down to the basement-level jail.

If the town fathers of Snowshoe weren't going to take charge of things there, well, Longarm would take over and conduct business the way he saw fit.

"I got a prisoner for you," he said to a sleepy-eyed, unshaven jailer who was presiding over a row of four empty cells.

"Not without the chief says so, you don't," the jailer told him.

Longarm gave the man a smile that had no hint of mirth in it. "Y'know," he mused out loud, "that's about the same thing this fella told me. An' I told him the charge was obstruction o' justice. You wanta see how that charge fits you too, neighbor?"

"Care to sign your prisoner in, Marshal? I got the book right here."

"Thank you. Thank you very much."

"Before you ask, Marshal, I don't know where the chief nor anybody else has got to. That's the truth. They didn't let me know 'cause they know I'll spill anything if I'm pushed about it. All I was told was if I had any questions or wanted to pass any messages I was t' do it through John here."

Longarm pulled John around to face him. "That's corroboration of the charge against you, mister. The Justice Department will see it so. You're looking at eighteen months to two years. Twelve to fourteen months inside, even with time off for good behavior. And that time won't be spent strolling around a park. You won't like what you find inside those walls. You truly won't."

John looked away and refused to say anything.

"Take your prisoner, jailer. And I hope for your sake that you know better'n to allow him loose."

"I understand, Marshal."

Longarm retrieved his handcuffs, and watched while John was locked into a cell. Then the deputy completed the paperwork that was necessary. By the time he was done Longarm felt weary. Aggie followed him quietly back up the stairs. She was acting like she was still shocked that Longarm had actually gone through with the jailing and the charge against the clerk.

Neither of them said a word as they went outside and headed for a cafe.

Chapter 22

"Paper, mister?" The kid was about ten years old, with carrot hair and enough freckles to share with half a dozen buddies. His clothes said he was poor, but his grin said he probably didn't realize it. Hell, he had a job to do, and therefore was in possession of all the prospects in the world. All the ones that counted, anyhow.

"Fresh news, son?" Longarm asked.

"Yes, sir. The *Snowshoe Independent*, sir. It comes out twict a week. This here one was printed just this morning."

"Help out with the printing too, do you?"

The kid's grin got bigger. "Yes, sir. Sometimes." He giggled. "When things go just right I've helped. That's how you can always tell."

"Then I expect I can take your word that things are as they should be, eh?"

"Yes, sir."

Aggie became tired of Longarm's playful conversation with the newsboy. She motioned that she was going on ahead, and swept off in the direction of a restaurant that she favored, leaving Longarm to catch up when he pleased.

"How much for this newspaper of yours, son?"

"The usual, mister. Two cents."

"A man couldn't hardly pass up a bargain like that."

"No, sir," the boy agreed.

Longarm handed the youngster a nickel, accepted his newspaper in return, and waved away the offered three cents change.

"Thanks, mister." The kid sounded sincere, and no doubt

was. But by the time Longarm winked at him, he had already turned away and was looking for his next customer. He wasn't wasting any time dawdling where all the readily available profits had already been reaped.

Longarm chuckled and wandered off in the direction Aggie had just taken, carrying his paper with him.

The restaurant she'd entered had a menu board outside advertising everything from elk steaks to smoked buffalo tongue and a good assortment in between. The lady lawyer had just walked past two other cafes that served such mundane articles as mulligan stew and cheese sandwiches. Apparently Miss Agnes preferred living somewhat higher on the hog than that.

"You certainly took your time," she complained once he had joined her at a corner table.

"Didn't know we was in all that big a hurry," he responded.

"I don't know about you, dear, but I happen to be hungry. I've already ordered, by the way."

"For both of us?"

"Yes, of course."

For some reason it irked him that Aggie was assuming she should, or could, take charge like that. "Oysters on the half shell, I s'pose," he grumbled. "Or is it a pâté?" What he was in the mood for was something solid and meaty, steak and potatoes, sausage and biscuits, something on that order. Definitely not any fancy-prissy crap like truffles and pickled quail eggs.

"I only wish oysters were available," Aggie said, missing his tone of voice and taking the question seriously. "But we won't get any fresh oysters in until the railroad is completed, I'm afraid."

"Such a pity," Longarm said with no particular sympathy.

"Yes, isn't it?"

The conversation wasn't going anywhere. Longarm retreated from it by leaning back and opening the local newspaper. He glanced at a bold headline in the upper left corner of the front page.

98

Then sat bolt upright with a frown.

"Damn!" he blurted out.

"I beg your pardon?"

"Damn," he repeated, loud enough this time that heads turned at the adjacent tables to see what was wrong. "D'you see what some sonuvabitch has gone an' done?"

Chapter 23

Longarm went outside and bought another newspaper. It was either that or wrestle Aggie for possession of the first one. By the time he came back to the table she was muttering and moaning and getting red in the face.

"But this isn't . . . this is . . . but these are all lies . . . all of it. Lies. This . . . this is terrible. Unconscionable. Disgusting. There isn't a word of truth in it."

"Hush," he told her.

"Don't tell me to hush."

"Fine. Miss Able, ma'am, with all due respect, ma'am, I do humbly request that you shut the hell up for a minute while I read this. All right?"

She glowered at him, but was too busy reading and groaning to do anything more about it at the moment. Every once in a while she would sit up straighter in her chair and yip a little or maybe squirm.

Longarm hurried through the article as well. And understood completely why she was so unhappy with what she was reading.

Hell, the headlines had been enough. "Wild Indians Threaten Massacre. Government Unable to Control Ute Tribe. Second Meeker Uprising Likely. Expert Warns of Dangers."

"Shee-it!" Longarm said.

The article beneath the bold headlines was even worse.

According to the author of the fabrications—Longarm knew the statements to be fabrications; probably Aggie knew them to be fabrications; probably they were the only two people who would ever read this newspaper who would know that, though—the Ute nation was on the verge of a general breakout and bloodletting. And the band of Utes imprisoned at Snowshoe was the advance guard for the war parties that were said to be gathering throughout the mountains.

Women, children, and all. Sure. You betcha. Anybody who would believe that crap, Longarm knew, didn't know anything about Indians in general or the Ute tribe in particular.

Unfortunately that category, those who knew next to nothing about Indians, included damned near everyone who lived around there.

The warnings were attributed to a "highly placed source with the government." Who didn't have his name mentioned anywhere in print, Longarm noted. Convenient. For somebody.

"Anyone who reads this will become hysterical when those people are released, Longarm," Aggie said. "They are sure to. Why, they will believe they are on the verge of disaster, that all of us are to be slaughtered."

"That sure seems t' be the idea," Longarm agreed.

"Whyever would some government spokesman say things like this?"

"What gives you the idea that somebody official said any o' this?"

"Well . . . this, of course. Right here, as you can see for yourself." She showed him her paper and tried to point to the offending paragraph.

"I read that part a'ready, Aggie. What I'm saying is, I don't reckon anybody official said anything like that."

"But . . ."

"Aggie, surely you learned by now that some folks will lie now an' then."

"But . . ."

"No reason why a man who'll lie to your face won't lie on paper too."

"I can't believe . . ."

"You know the fella that wrote all this shit?"

101

"Certainly."

"I think I need t' pay him a visit."

"I shall go with you. As soon as we've eaten."

"You can wait here if you like. Me, I want t' get on with it."

"But lunch is already here, Longarm. That's ours on the tray coming now."

Aggie surely did like her groceries, Longarm conceded. And she was just the sort who would refuse to help him find the newspaperman until she'd had her way. Which in this case would involve getting some grub down. He might just as well sit back and fill his own belly while he was waiting for her.

The meal she'd ordered turned out to be something with a foot-long French name. Longarm was fairly sure he'd never heard the term before. On the other hand, he didn't really need to. Once you cut through the fuss and fancification, what it came down to was a good old mulligan stew cooked and served inside a little bitty pie crust. He wondered if he ought to point that out to the lady, then decided it was probably better not to. Let her enjoy paying half a dollar here for the same kind of mulligan she could get down the street for fifteen cents.

"Hurry up there, would you?" he prodded. "We got work t' do, dang it."

"Don't rush me," she shot back at him. But she was hurrying in spite of what she said, he saw.

Chapter 24

"Ellis Farmer, I would like you to meet Deputy Marshal Custis Long. Marshal Long, Mr. Farmer is the editor of the *Snowshoe Independent*."

Deputy Marshal Custis Long scowled. Editor Farmer beamed with pleasure, either real or feigned. "How convenient," he enthused. "I was going to look you up this afternoon, Deputy. I hope to interview you about your, um, business here."

"Yeah. Real convenient," Longarm grumped. He felt no inclination to suggest that Farmer join Longarm's friends in the use of his customary nickname. "Did you write—?"

"Pardon me a moment please, Deputy. This will only take a second. Then we can talk as long as you wish." Farmer smiled and rubbed his hands together, and hurried out of the newspaper "office."

Calling the publishing site of the *Snowshoe Independent* an office was putting the best face on things, to be sure. It consisted of a tent, and a rather shabby one at that, with timber reinforcements at the corners and native stone laid down to fashion an uneven floor of sorts. The roof sagged, and in some places the canvas was so thin that the sun practically shined right through. Longarm suspected it would leak like so much fishnet when it rained.

Wooden crates were piled at the front to create a counter of sorts, and more crates and sturdy boxes were used as desks and chairs. Racks of metal type stood on sawhorses at the back of the tent, and a portable press rested on a stoutly constructed table, the only article of genuine furniture in the whole damned place. Longarm's impression was that the *Snowshoe Independent* was not a particularly prosperous enterprise.

Longarm pulled a cheroot out and lighted it. He hadn't taken time for an after-dinner smoke before now, and the flavor of the tobacco was especially welcome. There in public he didn't offer one to Aggie, and he thought the dirty looks he was getting from her might have something to do with that. He grinned and winked and blew smoke rings into the air between them.

"There, that didn't take long, did it," Farmer said as he breezed back in from his errand. "Would you care to sit down? This way, please." He took Aggie's elbow and guided her to a seat on a crate marked FloEver Ink.

"You can sit there, Deputy. But I would prefer it if you didn't smoke. Stinking, nasty things, cigars. I detest them."

"Do tell."

"Yes indeed. I find them quite vile."

Longarm took a closer look at the editor named Farmer. The fellow was thin and pale. He was of average height and wore a closely trimmed beard. His hairline was receding badly even though he was probably still in his twenties. There was something about him, though, that wasn't quite . . . normal. Nothing overt. Nothing Longarm could point to and say, "Hey, that's it." Just something that wasn't quite . . . right.

Fortunately that wasn't something that Longarm had to give a shit about. Ellis Farmer's problems, whatever they might be, were his own worry.

"You wanta know what I detest?" Longarm asked. He kept the cheroot trapped between his teeth and gritted his question around it.

"I take it you intend to tell me?"

"You take it right, Mr. Farmer. What I detest, mister, is newspaper articles that aren't true. An' that incite to violence."

104

"I agree with you most strongly," Farmer said. "Most strongly indeed. I certainly would never be able to abide anything like that either."

Longarm puffed slowly on his smoke for a moment. "That story in today's edition comes t' mind, Farmer."

"Which one did you have in mind?" The question was deceitfully bland. The man had to know good and well which story was in question here.

Longarm's eyes narrowed.

"About my clients," Aggie put in, apparently accepting Farmer's smart-ass response at face value.

"Oh, yes. My warning about the impending atrocities. Not that I expect any praise, you understand. I was only doing my civic duty to pass that information along. Protecting the life and property of one's fellowman is what any good newsman hopes to accomplish."

"Where'd you come up with bullshit like that?" Longarm snapped.

"Surely you can't mean—"

"Quit your playacting, Farmer. Why'd you print a string of lies like that? You must've had a reason, man. But damned if I can work out what it could be. Can't see any sense in it whatsoever."

"Lies, Deputy? What lies could you possibly mean?"

Longarm glowered at him. It was Aggie who answered the man. "There is no danger from the Ute tribe, Ellis. Certainly there is no danger from the band of frightened, innocent people I represent here. Now why in the world would you print a story saying all those awful things?"

"But those were not lies, I assure you. I was given that information by my source. I repeated the warning exactly as it was given to me."

"Bullshit," Longarm said.

"We won't accomplish anything if you insist on being rude," Farmer said.

"Fact remains, mister. Your story is bullshit. Dangerous bullshit at that. The sorta bullshit that causes trouble an' gets innocent people killed."

"Just what part of my story do you claim is, um, bullshit, Deputy?"

"Roughly speaking, I'd say it's the part between the first word an' the last one."

"I see. For instance then, you dispute what I wrote in my story about the massacre at the agency? About the Rev. Mr. Meeker and those other innocents being slaughtered? Was that bullshit, Deputy? Have I been misinformed? Did those deaths not actually take place?"

"You know that isn't what I was talking about, Farmer."

"Then perhaps you do not believe that young white women were . . . excuse me, Agnes, I don't mean to be indelicate in your presence . . . were raped by savages during that recent uprising. Did that not happen either? Is that what you disagree with, Deputy?"

"Damn you, you know—"

"But you claim that everything I wrote was false, do you not?"

"Mister, you're sitting here playing word games. Stupid ones, at that. I'm trying to see that the laws of this country are enforced an' that no innocent people, not white ones nor red either one, come to harm. Now what I want from you is nothing more than plain truthfulness. In particular, man, I don't want you getting folks worked up with a bunch o' lies that can't do anybody any good. You work folks up an' get 'em scared, the next thing they'll be shooting into the shadows. Gunning down the next Indian who walks by, just out o' the fear that you put into 'em. Innocent people can get killed, mister, an' all because of your stupid lies."

"And I say my story is not a lie, Deputy. Not the least part of it."

"That's a lie right there, Farmer."

"Prove it."

"All right, I will. Tell me who this high-placed government source is s'posed to be. If you can. Though you an' me both know that you can't."

"My source of information does exist, Deputy. And I challenge you to prove otherwise."

106

"Who is he, Farmer? Let's you an' me both set down an' talk to this guy."

"I can't divulge a news source, Deputy, nor can you force me to. Surely you understand that. Why, even suggesting such a thing constitutes . . . and I use the term advisedly . . . a violation of my First Amendment rights of free speech. I daresay the confidentiality of a newspaperman's sources of information enjoys every bit as much protection under the law as a priest's confessional disclosures."

"Bullshit," Longarm said.

"Do you know of any specific case law to dispute me, Deputy? Or do you, Agnes?"

Longarm's only answer was a scowl. Aggie frowned, but had to admit that if there was a case to cite she wasn't familiar with it offhand.

"You came here to dispute my story, Deputy. As it happens, however, *I* dispute *you*. I claim accuracy in my report and a public duty to distribute what I know so that innocent white families will not be taken by surprise and subjected to another massacre by red savages. Now if I may say so, Deputy, I am not in a mood to interview you right now. I frankly don't believe I could do so objectively. And you *know* I pride myself on my accurate and impartial reporting. So if you would excuse me, please?"

The son of a bitch stood up and gave Longarm a snooty look.

Lies. Every stinking bit of it lies. And they all three of them knew that it was all lies. Yet the bastard stood right there and looked them in the eyes with his own bare face hanging out and lied some more.

This was crazy, Longarm thought. Crazy as hell.

The really sad part of it was that there wasn't a damn thing he could do about it either.

Even if he could prove that every word in that newspaper story was a lie—and he sure oughta be able to prove that— he still couldn't do a damn thing to stop it. Because for some stupid reason nobody'd ever gotten around to making it illegal for a man to tell a lie. Not even in print. And wasn't that a damned shame, Longarm thought bitterly to himself.

He took a few last puffs on his cheroot and blew smoke in the direction of Ellis Farmer, then dropped the partially finished cigar onto the stone flooring and ground it out under his boot. With any kind of luck the smell of it lying there would piss Farmer off.

Longarm stomped out without bothering to tell the bastard good-bye or looking back to see if Aggie was following.

Chapter 25

Aggie was pale and, for the first time, seemed genuinely worried. "They could be killed, couldn't they?"

"The Utes?"

She nodded.

"Ayuh," Longarm agreed. "They could be. Just as bad, there could be others killed too. Other Indians killed if that article stirs people up too bad. Whites killed if the Indians retaliate. Something like this can run a long, ugly time if it once gets up a head o' steam, Aggie."

"I hadn't thought that . . . until now, Longarm, I've been regarding this whole thing as a game. A way I could show off and impress the people of Snowshoe. Oh, I've honestly wanted justice for my clients. But I hadn't ever thought that this, any of it, could be so deadly serious. But it is serious. It really is."

"Uh, huh."

"We need to find Chief Bevvy, don't we?"

"Him or somebody else. The mayor, judge, some-damn-body. We need to get this writ served, or at the very least get those Utes released from wherever they're being held. Gotta get them the hell outta these mountains for a spell, an' the quicker the better."

"Come with me," Aggie said abruptly. She turned and hurried away, Longarm trailing close at her heels.

The lady lawyer took him off the main street to a maze of narrow alleys that seemed to be passing as streets, with shacks crudely fashioned from packing crate slats pressed in on both sides, the footing uncertain because of the trash that was strewn everywhere. At night, Longarm suspected, this area would be quite the rat hole.

Snowshoe's tenderloin swallowed them whole, and he could smell cheap perfume and opium smoke, could hear grunting and weeping and the rhythmic creak, creak, crunch of steel bedsprings.

It occurred to him to wonder how Miss Agnes might have come to know her way around in this particular part of town.

"This way," she said, turning yet another corner. "In here."

He had to duck to pass beneath a lintel that still carried writing on it to show it once had been a part of some other object. No telling now what that might have been. He could make out the letters B, A, and N.

The inside of the hovel was dark even in mid-afternoon. Too dark for one's eyes to readily adjust. He failed to see Aggie stop in front of him, and bumped into her.

"I need to see her," Aggie said.

"Wait." The answering voice was deep. Longarm realized there was a man, presumably a guard, somewhere in front of them. It was so dark that he hadn't seen anyone, or even realized that he and Aggie weren't alone there.

There was a sound of footsteps, and then a rectangle of light appeared ahead as a door was opened and a burly form passed through it.

Longarm's Stetson kept scraping the ceiling, and he was tired of stooping. He took the hat off and was able to stand upright without bumping his head. His eyes began to adapt to the poor light.

"What are we doing here?" he whispered. Somehow whispers seemed very much in order at the moment.

"Shh. You'll see."

"Thanks," he said dryly.

"You're welcome."

He made a face, which Aggie couldn't see.

The wait only required a few moments more. The door was opened again, and this time the male figure stood there without stepping through. "She'll see you, Miz Able."

"Thank you, Parson."

Longarm had a pretty good notion that Parson, when spoken in this connection, would be a nickname and not a description. Most parsons would keel over in a dead faint if they were ever to get a look inside a place like this one.

"Yes'm," the voice said.

Longarm followed Aggie to the door and past Parson into the next room. His eyesight had returned well enough by now that he could see the guard. Parson had a face that was burn-scarred and twisted. The effect gave him an evil look, although that accidental appearance didn't necessarily have a thing to do with the way he really was. He might really be a pussycat. Still, such an intimidating look must have been quite an advantage to him in his present line of work.

Beyond the doorway the ceiling was higher. In fact, the room where they now stood was relatively normal, bordering on being quite nice. There were Oriental rugs on the floor, lamps in sconces on the walls, and furniture that was a trifle shabby now but which had once been quite grand.

Mostly, though, the room was dominated by a bloated old woman who seemed to be all fat and face powder. She was dressed in a fluffy pink lace wrap that enveloped her from her ears to the floor and beyond. She looked like she was floating in a pink cloud, with only her heavily powdered face exposed. Even her hands were lost somewhere inside the gown. Her hair was wispy and white. Longarm couldn't decide what her age might be. Old enough to call Methuselah sonny, perhaps.

"So nice to see you, dearie," she said to Aggie. Then she transferred her attention to the tall deputy who stood beside the lawyer. She nodded. "Nice to see you again, Longarm."

"Have we met?"

"Not formally."

"You have the advantage of me, madam." He smiled and brought his heels smartly together, bowing slightly from the waist as he did so.

"Always the gentleman, aren't you. I would refresh your memory, love, but I don't recall what name I might have been carrying at the time. It was in Tucson, I think. Or was it El Paso? No matter. We were not at cross-purposes. And I do remember that I liked you."

Longarm was damned well positive he had never laid eyes on the old harridan before this moment. He damn sure would've remembered her if he had.

On the other hand, it wasn't at all impossible that she might have seen him. He could've been pointed out to her. People who spent their lives on the shady side of things, as he assumed this woman surely did, tended to pay close attention to the lawmen who might someday come after them.

"What can I do for you two children?" the old broad asked.

Longarm left it for Aggie to answer, as this visit was her idea and she was the one who knew the woman. Longarm still hadn't heard a name attached to her.

"We're looking for Boo Bevvy," Aggie said.

"You might have a long wait then," the woman said.

"He heard Longarm was here and is hiding?"

"There are people who might want to give that impression, but the truth isn't so dramatic," the old bat told them. "Boo is off investigating the robbery, dear."

Longarm found it more than passing strange that neither woman seemed to find it necessary to specify which robbery they referred to. *The* robbery for some reason seemed to cover it.

"I should have thought of that," Aggie said.

"You can't think of everything, dearie."

"What about the mayor?"

"He's with Boo."

"And the judge?"

"At home by now, I should think. Or hiding out somewhere else if he believes our friend Longarm will be coming after him."

"Why would I do that?" Longarm asked.

"Because he ordered your prisoner released from the jail not ten minutes after you walked out," the old bawd said, and cackled. She seemed to find that amusing as hell. Longarm did not. "Now he and John and your jailer friend are all laying low. They're afraid of what you might do to them. But they've even more afraid of what might happen to everyone in these mountains if the Indians are turned loose, you see."

"I don't understand that," Longarm complained.

The old woman shrugged. "Rumors. There were rumors long before that newspaper article came out this morning. That fool Ellis Farmer's story only fanned a fire that was already burning."

"Do you know how the rumors started? Or who started them?"

"My dear man, I don't know quite everything that happens here. Even if I do pretend that I do."

"But the police chief isn't actually in hiding from me?"

"He will avoid you if he can. I doubt that Boo would risk a federal indictment and the loss of his reputation over it. Boo has his weaknesses, God knows . . . for which I am suitably grateful . . . but total stupidity is not one of them. Boo won't carry his game with you any further than he believes he can justify in a court of law if it should come to that."

Longarm nodded. "That's good to know. Thanks."

"I didn't go into all this for you, Longarm. I owe you nothing. I did it for my Agnes, bless her sweet heart. And mind you treat her nicely, Longarm, or I shall become cross with you. You wouldn't want that to happen."

"No, I don't believe I would," he said for the sake of avoiding an argument. The truth was that he didn't give a shit what this old woman did or did not like.

He was, though, grateful to her for whatever information she might pass along.

"Thank you, Sally." Aggie went forward and leaned down to give the old bag a buss on the cheek.

"My pleasure, dearie. Anything I can do, you know that."

"If you hear anything . . . like where my clients are being kept now . . . ?"

"Do you want me to find out for you?"

"Yes, please."

"Consider it done, dearie. My children will locate them wherever they are and get word to you as soon as I know."

"Thank you, Sally."

Aggie curtsied and left. Longarm nodded and followed her, out past Parson and on into the brightness of the alleys. He waited until they were well clear of that place— whatever the hell it was—before he spoke again.

"Her children?"

"That's what she calls the, um, people who work for her," Aggie explained.

"Whores?"

"Some of them, yes. And a few pickpockets, I think. Cheats and sharpies of various kinds. Plug-uglies and bullyboys. Even some genuine children, I understand, although I haven't any idea what nasty use she puts them to. She controls them all by way of opium."

"Nice sort o' friend to have."

"I defended several of her, um, employees once. Gratis. That was before I understood that Sally could afford to hire anything done she wanted. And I do mean anything. She's insisted on being my friend ever since. I wouldn't say that I've ever objected."

"No, I can see how you wouldn't."

"Do you recall that I told you I was independently well off?"

"Mm, hmm."

"Actually, Longarm, you just met my independence."

"Makes sense."

114

"Are you disappointed in me, dear?"

"Hell, no. Nothing wrong with a lawyer making an honest living. An' it kinda stands t' reason that a lawyer's honest living has t' be earned in the company o' folks that ain't always honest."

She smiled and took his arm. "You do understand. Good."

"You think this Sally really will find out where the Utes are being held?"

"Count on it."

"I'll feel a whole lot better once they're safely away from this country."

Aggie didn't seem to be paying attention to what he was saying. Instead she was woolgathering, smiling and humming a gay tune and allowing him to guide her while she held onto him and stared toward the sky.

"It's a shame there aren't any oysters available," she said out of nowhere.

"Run that'un by me one more time?"

She laughed. "It's really quite logical if you think about it, dear. Oysters? You do know, don't you, what they say oysters are good for?"

"Oh."

"Exactly. And we haven't anything more pressing to do tonight while we wait for Sally to tell us where Bray Swind and his people are."

"Oh," Longarm said lamely. Unless Agnes Able had all of a sudden had a revelation on the subject of how to please a man, Longarm suspected he was in for a long and none-too-pleasant evening.

The things a man had to do in the line of duty sometimes . . .

Chapter 26

Custis Long wasn't a man to complain. But . . . damn.

He lay beside a sweaty and contented woman whose passions had all been sated. He only wished he could say as much about his own.

Aggie was still lush. Still beautiful. Still a truly lousy fuck.

On the other hand, the rent there was cheap. And there weren't any other rooms available in town.

Quid pro quo, as the lawyers said. Which, he supposed, was just another way of saying Life. Oh, well.

He smiled, and tapped the ash of his cheroot into the dish they were using for an ashtray. As before, the dish was resting on the damp flat between Aggie's tits. Tonight, though, he was smoking alone. She was so limp and wiped out after coming eight, nine times in a row that she wasn't even interested in showing off her toughness by smoking.

Not that Longarm had had to go completely unsatisfied. Toward the end there he'd finally figured out that he could tighten things up some by having Aggie bring her legs together while he lay on top of her with his thighs positioned outside of hers. It had seemed awkward only to begin with. Best of all, it had turned a loose and sloppy experience into something considerably more enjoyable. And she'd liked it too. If there were going to be any more belly-to-belly encounters with the lady lawyer, Longarm figured to handle them just that way again.

116

Beside him, Aggie yawned and snuggled deeper into her pillow, even though it was much too early for going to sleep, at least in Longarm's opinion. Far as he could see, the night had plenty of time to run yet. And he was getting hungry again. Supper was hours past.

What the hell. He swiveled around on his side of the bed and swung his feet to the floor.

"Are you leaving?"

"Hey, I thought you were sleeping."

"Sleepy," she admitted with a smile. "But not sleeping."

"Thought I'd go out. Get a drink. Play some cards. I dunno."

"You'll come back here tonight?"

"Sure."

"Good. Wake me when you do. We can do it some more."

"Sure." It was a small lie and a polite one. He stepped into his balbriggans, pulled on his socks, reached for his shirt. "Say, Aggie, since you happen t' be awake, there was something I forgot t' ask you earlier. Then when I thought of it again you were snoring."

"Longarm! I couldn't have. Ladies do not snore."

"Breathing deep?"

"Much better," she said.

"Anyhow, when I thought of it again I thought you were asleep."

"Thank you."

"The question . . . if you'll give me time t' ask it now . . . is this. When you and that woman were talking about the police chief, you both said something about 'the' robbery. Like you should both know what robbery was being discussed. An' you can call me a pessimist if you like, but I'd find it real hard t' accept the idea that there's only ever been one robbery in a town the size of this one."

Aggie laughed, and reached over to find his hand and squeeze it. "Of course we have our fair share of crime, dear. We aren't a bunch of backward hayseeds, you know. As for 'the' robbery, well, that one was special."

"Mmm?" He did a quick-shuffle stomp with both feet to set his boots comfortably, and checked the position of the big Colt in its cross-draw holster. It needed an adjustment to the right of a quarter inch or so before he could consider it perfect.

"Our train was robbed," she said.

"Hell, woman, you don't hardly have a train for anybody to rob."

"There are a few miles of track, you know. From Brightwater through Snowshoe and a little ways further."

Longarm was aware of that. He'd walked in along the road-bed when he'd come to Snowshoe. Apparently the narrow-gauge railroad here was operating much like the Silver Creek, Tipson, and Glory line did, trying to run cars along what little track they had to raise some working capital while they finished building track.

"Anyway," Aggie went on, "we had our first train rob-bery the other day. It was quite exciting."

"What'd they do, hit the passengers for pocket money?"

"Oh, no, much more exciting than that. This was a serious robbery. They took a gold shipment."

Aggie seemed to think nothing about that, but Longarm damn sure did. There wasn't any refinery in Snowshoe. He was positive about that. If there had been, he would have seen and smelled it long before now. Hell, the only stamp mills that could be operating there were small-time affairs that disassembled into parts small enough and light enough to be packed in by mule. And without heavy equipment, why, you just plain couldn't reduce gold ores to anything compact and valuable. The kind of concentrate that could be produced in a camp at Snowshoe's stage of develop-ment was bulky and heavy in relation to value. That very problem was the reason investors were so eager to build narrow-gauge rail lines into the small mountain camps. But until that happened, the concentrates produced in places like Snowshoe were hardly worth stealing, unless someone was prepared to undertake a major freighting project as part of his getaway.

He explained as much to Aggie, but all she did was shrug. "I wouldn't know about that, dear. I can only tell you that the train was robbed and the gold, whatever form it was in, was stolen."

"That's crazy," he said.

"Bite your tongue."

"Pardon?"

"Please don't you ever suggest that criminals should wise up and change their ways, dear. Not in my presence. Why, where would us lawyers be if it weren't for craziness and cupidity and all those wonderful human failings. So please, dear, speak with respect about the people I hope to have as clients someday."

He laughed and pulled his coat on, finally settling the Stetson into position. "Don't wait up for me."

"I had no intention of trying," she assured him.

He bent and gave her a perfunctory peck on the cheek before letting himself out of the cabin. What the hell, he decided, just because she was a lousy lay it didn't necessarily follow that she was a totally worthless person. There were times when she was fairly pleasant company. That probably ought to count for something.

Longarm ambled off into the night in search of a glass of rye whiskey.

Chapter 27

There are some genuine verities in life, pillars a man can depend on no matter what else befalls him, and one of those is that regardless of how badly a man hates your guts, he will still be willing to take your money.

Longarm might not be able to get anything in the way of cooperation in Snowshoe, but he could buy whiskey and lose at cards as well as the next guy. The whiskey wasn't bad. His run of cards was terrible.

"Fold," he said. "Again." He dropped the five useless pasteboards onto the table and leaned back.

"I really should feel guilty about this," the man on his right said. "I don't, of course, but I ought to." The fellow was the big winner of the moment, and except for that seemed pleasant enough. He was dressed too nicely to be an underground laborer. Longarm guessed him as a storekeeper or the like. He played his cards cautiously but very, very well, riding the percentages rather than hunches. For him it seemed to work. For Longarm tonight nothing was working, not even bluffs. Better to fold and wait for the next deal on a night like this one.

Longarm sipped at his rye and spent a few moments looking around the smoky room. There was a good crowd on hand, but they weren't rowdy. In fact, they seemed almost subdued. The noise level in the saloon was low enough that conversations two tables away could be followed if anybody was interested enough to bother listening.

The next hand played out—the same fellow winning it—and the players declared a short break, most of them dispersing in the direction of the outhouse, the bar, wherever. The gentleman who was doing all the winning sat back in contentment.

"Is it always like this?" Longarm asked.

"If you mean am I always this lucky at cards, the answer is that I only wish it were so. If, on the other hand, you mean to ask if it is always this quiet, the answer is that I only wish it were so."

Longarm raised an eyebrow.

The man smiled and explained. "With everyone so solemn lately there has been hardly any absenteeism problem in any of the mines. Few hangovers, you see. No broken bones in fistfights or ears ripped off in brawls. None of that lately. I must say that I like that part of it."

"Any idea why it's so quiet?" Longarm asked.

"Oh, no question about that. It's because of the robbery."

"The train robbery?"

"But of course." Like it was inconceivable that any other robbery could be discussed.

"Why in the world would that make a whole town so fretful?"

"Very simple," the fellow explained. "The concentrates that were taken represent the entire output of the major employers here. That was supposed to be the profit that would allow the mine owners, who happen also to be the railroad investors, to complete construction of the rail line, you see. This one robbery won't be enough to sink us. But much more in the way of loss and there will be no railroad. And if there is no railroad, soon there will be no town. The mines will close and that will be the end of that, because our ore values have been declining. Plenty of value if we have heavy equipment to extract metal from the ore. Not nearly enough value at the present level of technology available to us. We have to have that railroad in place, you see, or eventually we will fail and Snowshoe will cease to exist

121

except as a curiosity. Other towns in the area too. We're all in the same sad situation."

"Serious," Longarm agreed.

"Absolutely." The gambler sighed and pulled out a pair of cigars. He offered one to Longarm, then accepted the light that Longarm contributed. "Thanks."

"Mister, I can promise you I'd be willing to swap a match for one o' these cigars any time you want," Longarm said. "Now this is what I'd call a smoke."

"I have them special made," the gambler admitted. "The secret is a bright-leaf filler. Expensive but worth it."

"Worth it," Longarm agreed. He was definitely getting the impression now that this fellow sitting beside him wasn't any small-town shopkeeper. That sort of curiosity, though, would only be satisfied if the gentleman chose to volunteer information about himself. One man simply didn't ask personal questions of another. "I'm surprised your shipment was taken," Longarm ventured. "Unless you're getting an awful lot of extraction outta your ore here. But then you just said that you aren't, otherwise the future wouldn't be in doubt like it is."

"Frankly, Deputy . . . it is no secret who you are, I hope you don't mind."

"No offense," Longarm assured him.

"Frankly, Deputy, we were more surprised than anyone. We thought it impossible that anyone would have an interest in the shipment. Its value would be stated in the tens of thousands of dollars, true, but its weight was a matter of tons. Much too heavy to be moved by any conventional means. Mule train, for instance. It would have required a string of a hundred thirty mules to carry it. We calculated that first thing. And believe me, there are not that many mules in these mountains that were unaccounted for on the day of the robbery. That was the first thing we looked into."

"Logical," Longarm agreed. He glanced around, but the other players hadn't returned to the table yet. None of them, in fact. Although he could see one of the men standing at the bar in conversation with someone else. And now that he was paying attention he noticed another seated at a different table, already engrossed in a new game there. It occurred to him that perhaps this was something of a setup. Just maybe he'd been seated beside this pleasant fella for a purpose? Not that he minded. Yet. But it was something to keep in mind.

"Freight wagons could carry that much weight, of course," the man went on, "but no wagons can reach the area where the robbery occurred. It simply isn't possible. Even so, we searched for wheel tracks. There were none."

Longarm grunted.

"We are at a loss as to how the concentrates were spirited away. And we are very much concerned that the thieves may successfully repeat their performance. Until we know how they did it the first time, we will have difficulty thwarting them the second time. If you see what I mean."

"I see what you're saying," Longarm admitted. "I'm not so sure I see what you mean. Not all of it anyhow."

The gambler smiled. "Good. You are as bright as we'd hoped you might be."

Longarm didn't know quite what to make of that remark, so he let it slide by.

"We . . . our little consortium of mine owners and railroad investors, that is . . . have mixed thoughts about your presence here, Deputy. I suspect you can understand that."

"Not particularly. Not unless you're doing something you oughtn't."

"Oh, no. Nothing at all like that, I assure you. No, our, um, concerns lie with the Ute Indians. You are here to give them the freedom to attack us. Naturally we resist that. The other side of that coin, Deputy, is that your expertise could be useful to us when it comes to arresting whoever stole our gold concentrates."

"Personally I don't see that there has t' be any conflict, mister. Mister . . . ?"

"Delacoutt," he said quickly. "Ames Delacoutt." He extended a hand to shake. Longarm introduced himself,

123

although that wasn't really necessary, as Delacoutt already had said.

"Anyhow, Mr. Delacoutt—"

"Ames. Please. There is no reason we should be at odds, Deputy. Please call me Ames."

"All right, Ames, as I was sayin', there's no reason we have t' sniff assholes an' snarl. You see, there's no danger from those Utes. I know you've been filled with all kinds of wild tales on the subject, but I'm here to tell you that once I get those people out of whatever confinement your local law has put them in, the first thing they'll want t' do is get the hell away from here. This time of year they'll be heading down to the flat country anyhow. They got no desire to stay up here. Won't want to come back till late fall. An' then they won't be wanting to bother you. Those people are like most any others, Ames. Do you leave them alone an' treat them with decency, they'll give you the same right back. They'll leave you be and not be a bother to anybody."

"Your opinion is not universal, Deputy."

"Neither is good sense, Ames. Which ain't to say that it shouldn't be, just that it isn't."

"Leaving the question of the Indians aside for the moment, Deputy, we were hoping we could, um, prevail upon you to help us solve our robbery problem."

Longarm puffed on the cigar Ames Delacoutt had given him. It was without doubt one of the finest he had ever had the pleasure of tasting. "Was there any mail taken in the robbery, Ames?"

The man frowned. "Not that I am aware of. Is that important?"

"Does your railroad have a contract to carry mail?"

Delacoutt broke eye contact with Longarm and began peering at his fingernails.

"What is it that you'd rather not tell me, Mr. Delacoutt?"

"The line doesn't, well, it doesn't actually have a charter yet. And no mail contract, of course."

"I see." And he did. No charter, therefore no insurance coverage. These boys were taking the whole sting from

124

that robbery. "I hate t' be the one t' tell you . . . though I suspect you already know it . . . but no federal law was broken in that robbery. This is something for your county law to handle."

"The county seat is Silver Creek."

"So?"

"Silver Creek people are not interested in Snowshoe's problems. The county sheriff was told about the robbery. We haven't seen a deputy up here yet."

"Which is why your town chief of police is out looking for something that's clearly outside his jurisdiction."

"Exactly."

"I was kinda wondering 'bout that."

"But you could—"

"Ames, let me set you straight about something. I can't march in an' throw my weight around when I don't have jurisdiction. This is a local crime, an' the only way I could get into it would be if the local law asked me t' help. I got the authority to cooperate, but only on specific request. Without that, man, my hands are tied. And, uh, judging from the look on your face, I'd say that you already been told all this. Why am I bothering?"

"We were hoping you might . . . make an exception? You would be handsomely compensated, I assure you."

"Bounty hunting? That ain't what I do, Ames."

"It wouldn't be that at all."

"Okay then. You want t' bribe me to exceed my authority."

"No!" Delacoutt yelped.

"Look, Ames, if you boys want me in on this, get your police chief t' stand in front o' me and ask for my help."

"If Boo Bevvy stands in front of you, Deputy, you'll serve that writ you are carrying, and we will have to turn a flood of savages loose on our women."

"I already told you, man—"

"And I don't believe you. All right? Is that clear enough? The federal government mollycoddles those red savages. Everyone knows that. Lo, the poor Indian. Well excuse

125

me for saying so, but Lo butchers white babies and rapes white women and scalps white men, and those of us who don't have to follow a party line on the subject would just as soon see Lo and all his relatives dead and buried. And that, sir, is the truth as I see it."

And it was too. The way this dumb, deluded bastard saw it, anyhow. At least he was being honest in his reaction. Longarm found it difficult to fault a man for that. And he had to admit that he would've felt the same himself if he believed what Ames Delacoutt did. The difference between them was that Longarm happened to know better.

"I'd be glad to help out with your robbery investigation, Ames," Longarm said. "But you know what you folks gotta do first."

"You force a hard choice on us, sir. If we don't give in to your demand, we face ruin. If we do, we face death. Thank you *so* much, Deputy." Delacoutt sounded bitter, and no wonder given the lies that he believed.

"Look on the bright side, Ames," Longarm suggested. "Maybe your town policeman will solve the train robbery. Then all you'll have t' worry about is the kind of so-called friend who'd lie to you about things like wild Indians. Who, in case you don't know it, are just as human as you and me, mister. Which means there are good ones an' bad ones an' in-between ones. Just like you and me and the lying SOB who filled you full of make-believe fears. Now you think about that, Ames. Me, I'm going to bed. Somehow my pleasant evening on the town ain't as fun right now as I was wanting. Thank you for the cigar, sir. And good night."

Chapter 28

It still wasn't all that late. Late enough, though, that Longarm was going to go back to Aggie's cabin and see if he couldn't sneak in without waking her. For sure he didn't want to put up with any more argument from the likes of Ames Delacoutt. Ignorance of that nature could curdle even the best whiskey inside a man's belly.

He walked the distance to Aggie's place in a matter of minutes, but paused outside. Whatever he might think about Mr. Delacoutt, he definitely had to applaud the man's taste in cigars. And the one Longarm was smoking wasn't close to being finished yet.

A cigar this good wasn't to be put out and kept overnight either. Smoke allowed to linger inside the body of the cigar would seep into the leaf and turn stale. By morning the flavor would be no better than that of any ordinary two-center. The way Longarm saw it, it would be damn near sinful to allow that to happen.

Better, he figured, to stand outside and finish his smoke before he went in to bed. Besides, the night air was clean and crisp, the feel of it good in his lungs.

There wasn't any porch or bench provided at the front of Aggie's cabin, but there was a roofed overhang on one side where firewood was stored dry and close to hand. At this time of year the wood pile was small, the past winter's use shrinking it down to little more than a cord or so, although when full it probably held closer to a dozen cords of split aspen. Longarm decided to step in there and perch on the stacked stove-lengths while he finished his cigar.

He wheeled and took the few steps necessary to reach the front of the covered area, then slowed to grope his way into the deep shadows.

He heard something. A gasp. And then the sound of a hammer being cocked.

Longarm's hand swept the Colt into his fist. But he had no target, dammit. Looking into the shadows of the woodshed was like peering into a coal bin at midnight. He knew there was something there, someone there, but he couldn't see who or where.

He himself, he knew, was silhouetted against the gray background of the night sky and the town lights.

But he still had no target.

He also had no time to think about it, dammit.

He dropped to one knee an instant before a gun barrel discharged.

A sheet of flame the size and shape of a cast net illuminated the shed for half a heartbeat of time. For that quick eyeblink of time he could see by the light of the muzzle flash.

Two men! There were two of them, dammit. Crouched. Staring. Wide-eyed. He hadn't time to think about whether he recognized either of them. Both held something. Dark, elongated objects. Shotguns, he thought.

Before he'd had time to assimilate the information the flash of light was gone.

A charge of heavy shot whistled through the air where Longarm's head had been a moment earlier.

He responded with his own answering fire so quickly that the sound of the shotgun's roar merged with the crisper, lighter report of his .44.

He was so close to the man the time of bullet travel was too short for him to be able to separate out the sound of his bullet striking flesh, but he heard a grunting cough that told him someone was hit. And likely hit in the body at that. The sound was that of breath being driven out of someone.

There were two of them, though. Two of them. By now the other one would be. . . .

128

Longarm threw himself to his right.

Even as he moved there was another muzzle flash not ten feet in front of him. Buckshot whipped and tore through the air, once again seeming to fly head high. An amateur then. He hadn't the knowledge or perhaps the nerve to place his shots with care.

Still, he'd had knowledge and nerve enough to get his shot off. There had been a second lightning sheet of fire and another rush of smoke.

Another half-seen, half-sensed image had burned onto the retinas of Longarm's eyes.

Two men still, but this time one of them kneeling. Falling? The image Longarm saw had been frozen in time. In the light of the muzzle blast a tableau had been displayed, colorless but in full dimension like a stereopticon view made life-size. Longarm's impression was that the one man, the one who was kneeling, was going down. The other was standing, in much the same posture he'd been in when the first blast had lighted up the shed.

Two men. Two shotguns.

More noise.

Behind? No, overhead.

Wood. Splintering wood. Collapsing. Damn!

The corner post of the woodshed had been lashed and shattered by the two shotgun blasts. Longarm heard the post crack and give way under the weight of the roof it supported.

He tried to gather himself. Wanted to spring to the side one more time.

Too late.

The roof came crashing down. He had time to raise his arms. Then poles and dry sod slammed onto him. Buried him. Knocked him flat beneath hundreds of pounds of roofing material.

Dust filled his nostrils, and he could hardly breathe.

The Colt was gone, swept out of his hand by the tremendous weight of the falling roof.

He could barely draw breath, and damn sure couldn't move.

He felt stunned. His senses were overloaded. The smell of sunbaked dirt was thick inside his nose, and the taste of it was in his mouth. His head spun from an impact that hadn't registered when he received it, but which he could feel now throbbing at the back of his skull. Hard sapling poles and heavy, broken sod crushed down atop him. His stomach churned sourly and he thought he might throw up.

Even so, he was struggling already to free himself from the fallen roof that could easily become a tomb. Without conscious thought he pulled and twisted and tried to scramble free of the weight.

He could hear. He could still hear. He could hear a footstep. And then another. A whisper. An anguished cry.

"You son of a bitch. You've killed him." There was pain in the sound of the voice. The pain of deep emotion. "He's dead, damn you. Dead."

If the guy who was speaking was who Longarm thought he was, and if this guy was saying what Longarm thought he was . . . well, good. Longarm only wished he'd gotten the both of them.

He felt on the ground for the Colt. Wherever it was, buried in the rubble or simply lost somewhere close by, he couldn't find it in the dark. He gave up and tried to work his hand back to his chest. He still had the derringer in his vest pocket.

He heard footsteps again. Movement. The sound of wood being thrown or kicked aside.

"Damn you, you son of a bitch." From the sound of the voice the live one was crying over the dead one. His voice was cracked and shaking. "Damn you to hell."

Longarm tried to reach the derringer. His arm came up short, held back by a section of wooden pole that was somehow wedged between Longarm's chest and his right arm. He jerked and pulled and twisted, but couldn't reach the damn derringer.

Try with the left, he told himself. Gotta get to it. Use the other hand.

He heard the sound of a gun hammer being cocked.

"Damn you."

He could see a little now. A dark figure loomed over him, in silhouette against the stars now that there was no roof. The standing, weaving figure held a short, stubby, double-barreled scattergun, its shape unmistakable. The man was crying. His shoulders shook, and he took a moment to wipe his eyes on the back of his coat sleeve.

"I'll send you to hell behind him, damn you," the man swore in a tremulous voice.

He raised the shotgun to his shoulder.

Longarm was still clawing with both hands. Trying to grab the derringer in his vest pocket. Trying to find the dropped Colt. Trying to wriggle the hell out of the way. Trying . . .

A muzzle flash illuminated the night once more.

The shotgun roared and spat its fire in a macabre halo of death and destruction.

Longarm snarled and cursed and continued his struggle.

After a moment it occurred to him that he was still alive to struggle. He stopped. Blinked.

There was a faint sound of scuffling. Very light. No more noise than that of a pair of rats mating in their nest. And then there was silence.

Longarm thought back.

The shotgun blast. It hadn't been directed down at him. Although that was certainly where the man had been aiming a moment before. Instead, he thought, the gun had been pointing harmlessly into the sky when it fired.

And there had been a half-seen blur of movement a scant fraction of a second before. Or had he only imagined that part? He didn't honestly know.

He tried to concentrate on listening to whatever the hell it was that was happening.

There was . . . silence. Absolute silence. Nothing at all now except the silence of the night and, somewhere far

131

away, the sound of a barking dog. A few seconds more and even the dog became quiet.

Longarm began pulling and squirming and clawing at the debris that trapped him there. Whatever the hell was going on, he would feel better about it all once he could stand up and move again.

Chapter 29

For long, agonizing moments Longarm could see nothing, hear nothing. Then a dark figure rose off the dirt floor of the woodshed. A man's figure seen in silhouette as before. Except now there was no shotgun. Longarm continued to struggle against his enforced confinement, desperate now to reach a gun—gun, hell, his knife would have been enough; that or a rock, the burning coal of a lighted cheroot, his own empty hands, any damned thing he could use as a weapon to defend himself—but the tangled debris held him captive as surely as manacles and leg irons could have done. The half-seen, half-sensed figure moved closer until it stood over Longarm while he continued to struggle futilely.

"Let me help you, Mr. Long." The man's voice was deep. Longarm had heard it before. He couldn't recall where or when, but he was sure he had heard this man speak before. "Here."

The fellow bent down, and a moment later Longarm could hear a grunt of effort. The tough roof poles, burdened by hundreds of pounds of sod, that held him pinned to the ground shifted and began to rise. One inch and then another. Slowly they were lifted clear.

"Hurry, please, sir. I don't have a good hold here."

Longarm wriggled and fought against his confinement. He twisted and pushed and managed to drag himself partway out of the mass of fallen material.

The unknown man who was helping him groaned and lost his grip. The poles crashed downward again with a clatter. But by then Longarm was free to his waist on one side, to mid-thigh on the other. He grunted and kicked, forcing himself out from under the weight of sod and dried wood. "There." He dragged himself free of the last of it, and felt himself being grasped by the shoulders and helped upright.

Lordy, but it felt good to be standing up again.

"Who the . . . ?"

"It's Parson George, Mr. Long," the dark figure answered. "I was coming to deliver a message to Miz Able. Seen what was happening. Sorry it took me s' long to do you any good, but I don't carry a gun. Never been any good with one of those things for some reason, so I quit carrying any. No point to it. So I had to sneak in close enough to jump that one. Sure hope you don't mind."

Longarm figured he could manage to forgive the guy. "You did fine, Parson. Thanks. Help me find my gun, please. And my handcuffs too if you don't mind. I've gone and lost them somewhere. I probably ought to cuff that fellow you put down there."

"No need for you to cuff him, sir," Parson said.

"No?"

"Not unless it's a regulation or something, sir. He's pretty much dead now. If that's all right. Sir." Parson sounded so dolefully apologetic that Longarm couldn't help wondering what would happen if he said it *wasn't* all right for the ambusher to be dead now. He put a rein on his tongue, though. He had the impression that poor ol' Parson wasn't much used to being joshed.

"I'm sure that's fine," was all that Longarm said on the subject.

It occurred to him that guns had been fired here, a roof had collapsed, and men had died. Yet there was no hint of acknowledgment of any of that from Aggie Able in her cabin. But then she'd already proven herself a timid woman once she was buttoned securely within her walls at night, hadn't she? "It's all right, Aggie," he said loudly enough to be heard inside. "Everything is okay now. Unbar the door

134

and hand us out a lantern, please."

Longarm didn't hear any movement indoors, but Parson must have. The bodyguard—errand boy too, it seemed—went around to the front, and came back moments later with an unlighted lamp. Longarm hadn't actually specified a light, had he? Just the means for it. He sighed and snapped a match head aflame.

Parson held the lamp while Longarm first found his Colt—it was lying in plain sight not two feet from where he'd been pinned—and then the handcuffs that had been jostled loose when the damned roof fell on him. He felt considerably better with the Colt back in hand, and quickly reloaded the lone chamber that he'd had time to empty. Only then did he and Parson move to the other end of the shed to examine the havoc they'd combined to create there.

"Nice shooting," Parson observed. "If I could do that I believe I'd carry a gun myself, Mr. Long."

Longarm's one bullet, hastily aimed on the basis of instinct and experience, had taken the first assailant square in the chest. His sternum had been crushed inward, no doubt stopping the man's heart in the middle of a beat. He would have been dead, or as good as, before his knees touched the ground.

Longarm had never seen the man before, he was sure. The fellow was dressed in town clothes, not a laborer's rough garb. He was nicely groomed, with a fresh shave and neatly trimmed hair. His collar was crisp and his tie carefully formed. Any veneer of civility ended there. A sawed-off shotgun lay partially underneath the body. Longarm examined both the gun and the man carefully. Of the two barrel tubes one remained loaded. The fellow carried no other weapons on him, not a revolver, not even a pocketknife. Odd, Longarm thought. The pockets held a perfectly ordinary collection of coins and tokens and lint. There was nothing to hint that murder for hire would have been a regular line of work, and no great amount of cash to show sudden good fortune. Longarm grunted.

"Let's take a look at the other one," he suggested.

Parson carried the lamp outside the remains of the woodshed—the roof at that end remained mostly intact—to the point where his leaping charge into the fray had carried him and his victim.

"Nice work yourself, Parson," Longarm said.

The bodyguard gave him a look of shy gratitude in response to the compliment. "Thank you, sir."

No wonder Longarm hadn't heard much in the way of grunting or scuffling. The man known as Parson had had nothing but a knife, yet had jumped a thug armed with a sawed-off shotgun. In the dark. Operating solely by feel. And had managed to dispatch the fellow so cleanly that the dead man's hair was barely mussed. The man had died so quickly that there was very little blood seepage around a stab wound that passed through his coat into his back, led carefully between two ribs, and almost certainly had punctured the heart with unerring aim. It had to have found the heart, in fact, or there would have been quarts of blood soaking into the soil for yards around. As it was, there had been no more blood loss than a single handkerchief might wipe away. This one had died almost as quickly as the man Longarm had shot. It was impressively nice knife work, and Longarm had truly meant the compliment he'd given.

Longarm checked this body too, but found nothing exceptional in any of the pockets. The only weapon had been the shotgun—and come to think of it, he realized now, neither ambusher had carried extra buckshot shells with them; their total ammunition supply seemed to be the two charges each carried loaded into their guns. That made no sense to him whatsoever, not if either man knew what he was doing there tonight. Moreover, the clothing and personal possessions were consistent with what any town dweller might have when out for an evening stroll. Damned odd, Longarm thought.

"There's something on the ground over here, Mr. Long," Parson said. "I c'n see something shiny over beside the cabin, sir."

"Let's have a look." Longarm got to his feet, the cartilage in his knees popping, and followed Parson and the lamp back underneath the precariously balanced shed roof.

He whistled softly under his breath when he saw what Parson had spotted in the gleam of the lamplight.

"Not real friendly, huh, Mr. Long?"

"Not real friendly," Longarm agreed.

In addition to their shotguns, the recently deceased had carried a few other items with them when they came to call.

And the fact that they'd come without extra ammunition no longer seemed quite so silly. Hell, they hadn't expected to use those guns for anything tonight.

They'd expected fire to do all the dirty work for them.

What they'd left tucked beside a low pile of split aspen were four tins of coal oil. Each of the tins held four, maybe five gallons of highly flammable liquid. More than enough to douse the door and windows of Aggie Able's cabin, and start a conflagration that would kill the occupants of the place from oxygen deprivation long before the walls and roof might collapse in flames.

In addition to the coal oil, they had come thoughtfully equipped with a brand-new box of lucifers. The sandpaper scraper-panel glued to the side of the box was unblemished. No match had yet been struck there. Longarm grimaced and turned his head to spit. It was only coincidental that he happened to spit in the general direction of the nearer of the dead arsonists.

Longarm was a practical man, though. Before he moved away he retrieved the box of matches and helped himself to a pocketful. He offered the rest to Parson, and got a chuckle in return. "No thank you, sir, I don't smoke."

"Good for you, man. It's a nasty habit. Expensive too. Wouldn't stand for it myself except that it tastes so damn good."

"I might be able to sell that lamp oil to somebody, though," Parson suggested hopefully. "If you don't have a need for it, that is, sir."

137

"Help yourself."

"Thank you, sir."

"You wouldn't happen t' know who our visitors were, would you?"

"No, sir," Parson said. "They aren't from Snowshoe, I can tell you that. There isn't man, woman, nor child who lives here that I haven't at least seen b'fore, sir. They might not've seen me, Mr. Long, but it's part of my business to see and to know . . . things. If you see what I'm saying, sir."

Longarm did see. He nodded. This man who moved so fearlessly in the night was that fat old woman's eyes and ears. Parson was much more than merely a bodyguard to her.

"And I can tell you for sure, sir, that they aren't from around here."

Longarm kneaded his chin and pondered that.

Like nearly everything else connected with this deal, it made no sense.

It was the people of Snowshoe who were supposed to have a hard-on for him, dammit. Who were supposed to be so scared about the possibility that the Utes would be released from confinement and go on a rampage. Yet when somebody tried to kill him, it wasn't anybody from Snowshoe at all who made the attempt, but some strangers that nobody around there knew.

No, he corrected himself. Strangers that weren't from there, maybe. But that didn't necessarily mean that *no*body around there knew them.

*Some*body did. Somebody in particular. Otherwise they wouldn't have come to be there at the cabin with their full tins of lamp oil and their fresh box of matches. And, oh, yes, with their murderous intent for those otherwise-innocent items. So some-damn-body around there knew them.

The question was: Who? And why?

Longarm helped himself to a cheroot, the fire to light it provided courtesy of the late arsonists. His own smoke didn't taste as fine to him as Ames Delacoutt's cigar had— helluva stroke of good fortune that he'd wanted to finish that smoke instead of going straight inside and to bed; otherwise those handsomely dressed young men might have succeeded in their mission—but the nice part was that he was still alive to enjoy it.

"You said something about it being a message that brought you here tonight, Parson?"

"I wasn't gonna forget, sir."

"No, I don't believe you would have. The point is, why don't we go inside and see if we can't get Miss Aggie t' find us something to wet our whistles with whilst you deliver your message. Don't know 'bout you, but this kind o' work gives me a thirst."

"I'd consider it a honor, sir, a real honor if a gentleman such as yourself would sit an' have a drink with me."

"And I'd consider myself one sorry sonuvabitch if I refused to have a drink with a man who'd just saved my bacon. Lead the way, Parson, an' the honor will be mine."

Chapter 30

Parson seemed uneasy in the lamplight indoors where his facial disfigurement was so completely on display. Longarm turned the lamp low, and helped himself to a pair of drinks from Aggie's supply in the office half of the cabin. The lady was keeping herself out of sight for some reason. Frightened half out of her wits probably, Longarm suspected. And that was just because there'd been gunfire outside her walls. She had no way to know that she had barely escaped an ugly death by fire.

"To your good health, Parson," Longarm said, toasting the big man.

"Thank you, sir."

"My pleasure."

They both drank. Parson seemed pleased.

"Before we get down to business," Longarm said, "I know this isn't customary. But we've been through a good bit together tonight. I was wondering, Parson, if I could ask you a personal question."

The man touched his cheek, feeling of the scarred and puckered flesh there. He shrugged and nodded. "If you really want t' know, I suppose there's no reason why I shouldn't tell you. This happened t' me when—"

"Whoa!"

"Sir?"

"I wouldn't ask a thing like that, Parson. None o' my damn business, an' likely painful for you t' have to call back to mind." He smiled. "Not that the other is any of my business either. But what I keep wondering on, Parson, is how you came by a name like that. I mean, I'm real sorry. I know better'n to pry into another man's personal life. But the question just keeps fretting at me, if only because of how poorly it seems to fit you. And, uh, you can now tell me t' shut up and tend to my own knitting. I won't take any offense an' will apologize for butting in where I got no call t' be."

Parson chuckled and shook his head. "This name? That's all you're wanting t' know? Aw, I don't mind telling you 'bout that, sir."

Longarm leaned forward and topped off Parson's glass with a shot of Aggie's fiery applejack, then helped himself to a freshener too. The liquor—calvados had she called it?—wasn't rye, of course. But it kinda grew on a fellow.

"You see, sir," Parson said, "an' I hope you understand, you bein' an officer o' the law an' everything, I hope you will understand that I don't mean to give no offense to you no more'n I took any from your question. You do understand that I hope, sir?"

Longarm nodded.

"Anyway, sir, the thing is, I kinda got a temper, sir. Which I know may surprise you but is true. An' every now an' then I kinda through no fault o' my own wind up in a lockup. And when I do, well, there's always reformers around that don't have anything better to do than what they think is good. I expect you know the type, sir."

Longarm nodded again and took a small swallow of the applejack.

"So when I get myself in trouble, sir, there's always some rich reformer asshole around to take a look at my face an' say what a raw deal I've got an' so it ain't my fault what I done, whatever it was that time, but society's fault for bein' mean to me, an' next thing you know these reformers are looking for some excuse to turn me loose. So what I do once they get worked up to a certain point, see, is I drop down on my knees an' shout a few hallelujahs an' amens and such an' let 'em see how I been saved through their good works. And then I start in to preaching at the other prisoners all

141

around me, you see. Which o' course is where the name Parson comes from. 'Cause I mean I surely do preach at these ol' boys. I give it all I got an' then some. And what all this does, see, is it makes everybody except the reformers real mad. The prisoners get pissed off because they want some peace an' quiet in their cells, not to be preached at day an' night by some idiot that don't know any more'n they do. And the guards and coppers . . . 'scuse me, but I expect you've heard the term before now, sir . . . anyway, they get pissed too because their jail is a real unhappy place where fights an' riots could get started an' people get hurt. Which they wouldn't much mind, o' course, except it might be one o' them that does the gettin' hurt. So at that point, sir, I got all those reformers wanting me sprung an' I got the other prisoners wanting me away from them an' I got the sheriff or chief of police or whoever wanting me the hell out o' his jail an' . . . ." He grinned. "Somehow it all seems t' work out, sir."

Longarm threw his head back and roared. "Damn me, Parson, if you aren't a likable son of a bitch. Have another drink. Then I suppose we'll have to get serious and you can give me the message Miss Sally sent."

Parson added a wink to his grin when he leaned forward to collect that promised refill. Longarm didn't believe for a minute, though, that the fellow had been lying. Not a bit of it, by damn.

Chapter 31

The information provided by Snowshoe's lady crime boss proved to be mundane stuff. Not that Longarm was complaining. If it hadn't been for that, Parson would not have been approaching the cabin when he had and the arsonists might have gotten lucky. Longarm didn't particularly want to believe that they would have. But he conceded the possibility, and was grateful to Parson for the way things had turned out.

The message sent by Sally said that the old woman had been able to determine who was guarding the captive Utes—there were four names, none of which meant anything to Longarm—but not where the Indians had been taken. Yet. Three of the four guards were regular customers of Sally's enterprises. She expected to learn more about the Indians as soon as any one of the guards came in for a little off-duty relaxation.

Longarm thanked Parson for the information, and asked him to carry the thanks back to the fat woman as well.

"Glad to do that for you, Mr. Long. Oops. I remember. You don't have t' tell me again." He smiled and corrected himself, as Longarm had begun to pester him to do. "Not mister, just Longarm 'twixt friends, right?"

"Right," Longarm said.

Parson chuckled and scratched behind his right ear. "Damned if I ever thought I'd have a deputy Ewe Ess marshal for a friend, though."

"Some of us are close t' being human."

Parson laughed and stood, reaching for his hat.

"One more drink before you go back?" Longarm offered. After all, it was Aggie's liquor he was giving away, so why not pour with a liberal hand.

"Thanks, Longarm, but I'd best get along. I got things to do. People to see." He winked. "Even if they don't know it at the time."

As a lawman who in theory was supposed to be about as interested in ethics and morality as in the strict letter of the law, Longarm supposed he should have been shocked or outraged or something. After all, this man in front of him was an admitted sneak and eavesdropper and window-peeper. And damned handy with a knife as well. No telling what other criminal qualities went along with those things. Longarm's practical side, though, made him think mostly that Sally had a valuable employee in his new friend Parson. And a likable one.

Longarm saw Parson to the door.

"Would you like me to send someone over to take care of those bodies, Longarm?"

"I suppose the police will have t' be notified," Longarm agreed.

"Aw, you ain't gonna catch 'em out that easy. They all know to stay clear of you. But I can get the barber . . . he's our undertaker too . . . I can get him to send somebody an' pick up the stiffs. They'll get around to finishing the paperwork after you've gone."

"I'd appreciate that, Parson. Thanks."

"Glad t' help, Longarm. G'night." Parson smiled and touched his forehead and disappeared into the night.

Longarm blinked. Parson really was very good. One moment he was there. The next he seemed not to be. Longarm happened to know the trick of it, so he wasn't quite as startled as he might have been. Anyone unfamiliar with the techniques of moving soft and silent in the dark would be scared spitless of anyone as good at it as Parson. Even so, Longarm gave credit where it was due, and silently saluted Parson for the fine performance, waving toward

144

where the man pretty much had to be before Longarm turned and went back inside the cabin.

He could hear a subdued laugh behind him as Parson acknowledged that he'd been caught out fair and square.

Aggie looked annoyed. "You certainly took your time about seeing to my welfare," she complained.

"You weren't hurt."

"I was frightened. And what have you done about that since you came back inside? Nothing, that's what. Absolutely nothing."

Longarm shrugged. All the danger had been outside and nothing had really come of it, so what was she worried about now? He failed to see why she was so fussed up.

Aggie looked like she was in a humor to pout and then expect him to jolly her out of it. The problem was that Longarm wasn't in a mood to do the jollying she so obviously wanted. Instead he told her in a dry and straightforward manner about the would-be arsonists.

"Those two won't be causing trouble anymore," he concluded, "but there's nothing to say that a good idea gone wrong can't be tried the second time."

"What's that?"

"What I'm saying is that just because these two didn't manage to murder the both of us tonight, it don't necessarily follow that there won't be another two available t' make another attempt. I mean, there's plenty of coal oil in the stores here an' plenty more matches. What I'm saying is that you and me will both be safer someplace else until this thing is over and done with. Someplace where I won't have to worry about going to sleep an' leaving you undefended." He was already reaching for his bag. "What I'm saying, Aggie, is that you'd best get dressed 'cause we got t' go find rooms."

"If we go to the hotel we won't be able to stay together," she pointed out. "Here we can at least pretend that you are sleeping in my front room . . . and thank goodness the hotel wouldn't accept you the other day . . . but if we take rooms

145

there now we couldn't possibly stay together any longer."

Longarm had already thought of that. Hell, it was one of the reasons he was looking forward to having to move in the middle of the night. Pretty though she was, in bed Aggie was still more trouble than she was worth. "I know that, pretty lady, an' I'll be losing sleep from not bein' near you. But I won't do nothing t' harm your reputation in town, an' I won't let you come t' other harm neither. Better we split now."

She gave him a kiss, her peevishness of a moment ago dissipated now, and began to dress, tossing instructions over her shoulders as to what bag he was to fetch for her and from where, what drawer to empty into the bag, and what case to get down from the top of the wardrobe. Very much more and Longarm figured they'd have to hire a pack train to carry it all.

"You don't have t' take everything you own, y'know. After all, Aggie, you'll still be in town. Be safe enough for you t' come back in daylight and fetch whatever doesn't get carried with you tonight."

She held up a silk scarf, draped it experimentally at her throat, and inspected the look of it in the bureau mirror, then frowned and threw it back into the drawer in favor of another. "You don't know much about women, do you, dear?"

"No," he admitted, "I s'pose I do not."

Chapter 32

It seemed fairly incredible after all that'd happened already during the evening, but it wasn't yet midnight when Longarm got Lawyer Able settled in at a lady friend's house—she'd pointed out that there was no reason for her to pay a hotel's rates when she did have friends she could stay with a for a few days—and was free to once again look for lodging in Snowshoe.

"Nothing's changed," the same supercilious son of a bitch of a hotel clerk said when Longarm reached for the guest register. "We still don't have any room at the inn. Marshal." The man gave Longarm a repeat look at a smug smirk too, just like the first time.

"Something's changed," Longarm said softly. He turned the book around and flipped it open, paging through in search of the next line open for an entry.

"We have no room for you here," the clerk said curtly.

Longarm stopped what he was doing. His face had become as still as a death mask, and his eyes bored cold and bleak into the desk man's.

"I don't . . . you can't force . . . I, I mean . . . ," the clerk sputtered.

Longarm reached slowly forward, his hand moving with calm deliberation. The clerk watched it as if mesmerized, the way a chick will with utter fascination watch the deadly approach of a snake. The clerk gulped for breath but did not think to pull away.

Longarm touched the knot of the clerk's tie. Gently. Very gently. He tugged it a fraction of an inch to one side, straightening it so that the knot was symmetrically centered between the wings of the man's collar. Just as slowly as he had reached out, Longarm withdrew his hand. And looked the clerk square in the eyes. "The thing that's changed," he said in a voice pitched so low that the clerk had to strain to hear it, "is that tonight you *will* give me a room."

The man swallowed. Hard. His breathing had become rapid and shallow, and he looked and acted like a man who had just completed a long-distance run. Or a man who had just walked the edge of an abyss and lived to think back on how good life and living can be. He licked his lips nervously and shuddered. "Yes," he whispered. "Sir."

"Thank you," Longarm said without lowering his stare.

"Would you . . . if you . . . that is, uh, sign . . . just sign . . . please?" He hastily fumbled along the counter to round up a pen and ink bottle, and pushed them in front of Longarm. "Please. Sir."

Longarm nodded solemnly, and finally dropped his glance so he could see the register to sign it.

By the time he was done with that the desk clerk had a key in front of him. "It's the best I have available. Sir. Honestly."

"Thank you."

"My second best room in the whole house."

"Thank you."

"On the top floor, it is. Number . . . um . . . oh, God, I can't remember. Sweet Jesus, don't shoot me, mister. It's . . . it's . . ."

"Calm down, man. It's written right here on the tag. And nobody's going to shoot you. Now calm yourself down."

"Yes. Thank you. Thank you very much, sir, thank you." The man looked actually relieved to hear that Longarm wasn't planning to cut him down right then and there.

Sometime, Longarm mused, he was gonna have to remember to get a look at himself in a mirror when

148

that sort of mood came on him. Except the only way he could think to do that would be if he was playacting, and so it probably wouldn't be the same. Sure made him wonder sometimes, though, what he looked like when he got really pissed off and folks started acting like this fella afterward.

Longarm accepted the key and bent to pick up his things.

"I . . . almost forgot, sir. There was a message. Although I did tell the lady I wouldn't be seeing you. Which I didn't know at the time . . . you understand?"

"What's the message?"

"The, um, guest, the lady, in my best suite? Number thirty-one, sir, two doors away from you. She, uh, asked that you be informed of her arrival, sir. And invited to, um, call upon her. At your convenience. Sir."

Longarm frowned. He'd just left Aggie at her friend's place, so it wasn't her. The only other woman he could think of meeting in this town was Parson's boss, Sally. And she sure as hell wouldn't be setting up shop in a legitimate hotel like this one. "Does this lady have a name, mister?"

The clerk looked like he was ready to faint. "Why, it is Miss Skelde, sir. She said you would be expecting her?"

Longarm frowned again. Skelde? Who the hell was this woman named Skelde? It took him several moments before he made the connection. Leah. That white-hot filly whose company he'd enjoyed down in Glory. Skelde was her last name. Sure it was. He'd forgotten all about her. And about the fact that she'd mentioned something about maybe coming to Snowshoe eventually. Apparently "eventually" happened sooner rather than later around there.

"Number thirty-one, you say?"

"Yes, sir. And you are to call on her at your convenience, sir. She emphasized that point. At your convenience."

"Thanks." Longarm carried his gear up the staircase to his room. Everything he remembered about Leah said that it wasn't at all too late for him to pay his call now. He'd just stop in his own room long enough to drop his things

149

there and give himself a quick washup—he hadn't had a bath since the last time he slipped and slid his way through Aggie's cavernous flesh—then pay his respects to the lovely Leah.

Chapter 33

This was better. This was the way it was supposed to be. Longarm stretched, feeling loose and content now, and pulled Leah tight against his chest, her breasts warm and soft against his sweat-filmed skin.

It was amazing, he realized. Point by point and item by item, anybody taking a close inventory would have to say that Agnes Able was far and away the more desirable of the two women.

Aggie was younger, prettier, better built. Likely smarter too if it came down to it. Certainly the more decent and respectable of the two. After all, Aggie was a lawyer. Leah was a former whore trying to make her fortune by indulging the vices of men.

Yet there wasn't any question which of the two genuinely lovely women Longarm enjoyed being with. In bed Aggie was selfish and petulant and basically inept. Leah was as giving as she was knowledgeable. And that right there was the biggest difference between them. Aggie took without a thought to giving. Leah wanted to give back at least as much as she got. Longarm was damned glad to be where he was right now.

"I like it when you look at me like that," Leah whispered.

He raised an eyebrow. "An' how would that be?" he asked.

"I don't know how to explain it. Like you just were doing." She smiled. "There! You're doing it again."

Longarm grinned and kissed her. "I dunno, woman. You might be 'bout half crazy." Her hand crept between their bodies to find his cock and gently fondle it. "A nice kind o' crazy, that is," Longarm amended.

His breathing had barely returned to normal after the first passions of greeting were spent. Now Leah was wanting to start all over again? He sure as hell hoped so. In fact, if she hadn't been the one to suggest it, he would've.

She was freshly bathed this evening, and smelled of soap and scented powder and a particularly delicate perfume fragrance. Her hair smelled as clean as her flesh, and her body was silky smooth and carefully shaven. Or plucked, however it was she managed to keep herself bald down there. Whatever the method, and however odd the appearance, the overall effect seemed worth the trouble. It gave an impression of extraordinary cleanliness. Felt nice too, by damn.

"Shall I whisper to the sleeping giant, dear, and see if I can arouse him?"

"Feel free, ma'am," Longarm said with a wink.

Leah sat upright, bending to give him another kiss. Then she moved slowly down, dragging her nipples across his body. Once she reached his waist she stopped and lowered herself to the bed again, spooning herself to him face-to-belly while she lay on her side. He could feel her breath hot on his damp cock. If the purpose of this was simple arousal, well, she'd already managed that much and more. He was hard as marble again, as wound up and ready as a boy in his teens sniffing after his first piece.

Fortunately the lady had more in mind than arriving at a hard-on.

She sighed happily as she leaned forward and began to run her tongue lightly up and down his shaft.

Longarm groaned and shifted slightly, rolling onto his side to make himself more comfortable. As if it might be possible to be any more comfortable than this. He smiled.

Leah's hairless pubis was there in front of him only inches from his eyes. He gave it a good looking over, and decided he still couldn't figure out if she shaved her bush or plucked it. The skin of it was soft and smooth. Moisture glistened in the lamplight where it seeped from the pink folds of her pussy.

And there were some things a woman might fake, but not this. Longarm could see Leah's own growing arousal in the way the lips of her snatch pulsed and fluttered and grew ever more wet as she licked and nibbled and sucked on his cock.

He could feel the heat of her mouth surround him and draw him inside her. He could see the responses of her body there before him.

It was interesting, he thought. And a damned friendly thing to do too. He chuckled, feeling suddenly very fond of this woman, and grateful to her for reminding him of what a woman could and should be. He closed his eyes then and leaned forward himself just a little. There wasn't very much needed. His tongue found the spot he wanted, and he felt Leah go loose and melt all the closer to him once they were locked head-to-crotch with each other in a French sixty-nine.

Leah was clean and smelled of jasmine, and her flesh tasted sweet. He nuzzled the pink, tender places, found the tiny button he wanted, and began to concentrate on it. The warm body that was pressed against his stiffened as the tensions rose inside her. Then with a loud cry of release she spasmed, clamping her thighs tight together and arching her back. Longarm waited until she was done with the overwhelming sensations, then gave her a brief, loud kiss on the cunt and lay back so Leah could concentrate on things at her end. Or his, depending on how one wanted to look at it.

If he thought she was good before, he hadn't known the half of it. It was as if Leah had been turned loose of all restraints. As if she wanted to prove herself the best there ever was.

She was like a great, hot, eager cat. Sucking. Touching. Taking Longarm deep into herself and holding him there.

Drawing on him so hard it was as though she wanted to keep him there once she got him where she wanted.

Longarm made no effort to guide her. But then he didn't need to. Leah knew his body better in some ways than he thought he did. She knew, and she was not shy about using her knowledge. She played his cock and his balls and all the nearby nerve endings like a superb musician might play a fine instrument. She built him until the intensity of his pleasure approached the fine line that separates pleasure from pain, until Longarm himself was not sure if what he was feeling was one or the other, until he knew only that he wanted this to last forever even if it was pain he was receiving.

Nothing lasts forever. Not even pleasure. Especially not pleasure. He exploded. He convulsed, his legs and belly contracting with the power of the ejaculation, and jets of hot fluid spewed out of him into Leah's own heat.

He cried out, and she was there to pet and soothe and comfort him. He hadn't even realized that she'd left his cock, but now she was bent over him, her eyes wide and moist and caring, and she was smiling as she ran a hand over his cheek and smoothed the hair back from his forehead and dragged a fingertip along the sweeping flow of his mustache, first on one side and then the other.

"Nice?" she asked.

"Don't you never do that t' anybody old," he said.

"What?"

"Takes a healthy heart t' not explode from anything that powerful." He winked at her. "Course it'd be a helluva way to go. Worth it."

She laughed and kissed the ball of her thumb and transferred it onto his lips. "Can I get you anything?"

"What'd you have in mind?"

"Whatever you want. Personally, I'm hungry. I didn't go out for supper this evening. I was afraid I might miss you if you came. Now I'm famished. I thought I'd ring down and have a late supper brought up. You're welcome to join me."

"Couldn't do that without people knowing you had a visitor," he said.

Leah smiled and shrugged. "Dear Longarm, my reputation could hardly be tarnished any further. And I earned every bit of it too. So don't worry about that. Now what would you like? A steak dinner with all the trimmings?"

"What will you be having?"

"Green salad, a little fruit, perhaps a pastry."

He made a face.

"Steak for you, dear, lettuce for me." She left the bed, her movements lithe and sure, and tugged the bellpull, then reached for her dressing gown. Longarm got up too. This best room in the hotel was nice and it was good-sized, but it wasn't any suite. Anybody at the door would get a good look at the bed too. He had time to dress before a sleepy-looking bellboy showed up.

Leah gave their meal order, and asked for a carafe of coffee and a magnum of champagne to be brought up while the food was being prepared.

"Carafe, mum?" the bellboy asked. "I thought that was a animal with a long neck."

"A carafe is a covered pot, son, something to keep the coffee warm in."

"Oh, that kinda carafe. Yes, mum, I'll get you one right up."

"Thanks."

Past Leah's shoulder the boy gave Longarm a look of blatant envy before he wheeled and trotted off about his duties. Longarm waited until he was gone, then winked at Leah. "What you wanta bet he has wet dreams about you for the next six months?"

"Only six months?" she exclaimed. "That's insulting. Wait until he comes back. I'll let my gown fall open. About, oh, this much?"

"Hussy," he said with a laugh.

"Indeed I am, you lucky man."

"Indeed I am that," he agreed.

Leah went to the dressing table and began brushing her hair. Longarm pulled out a cheroot and lighted it. "You said you didn't go t' supper for waiting for me? How'd you know I'd show up?"

"Why, you had to, of course," she said over her shoulder. "After all, dear, you are the only reason I came to Snowshoe."

"Mighty flattering, Leah, but you already told me before that you were comin' here anyhow. Caught ya."

"Laugh if you want, but it happens to be true, dear. I told you earlier that I would be coming to Snowshoe to look for a possible business site. Well, I won't be wanting one of those now. Not here. So why else would I come except to see you." She continued brushing her hair.

"You really don't have business here now?"

"Of course not. I may be a silly, simpering female the way you men look at it, but I am no fool when it comes to investment. And the smart money in this county says Snowshoe and these other high-country camps are going to fizzle out just as quickly as they boomed. Unless I want a short-term profit, which would be no profit at all, I've been advised to stay along the right of way of the Silver Creek, Tipson, and Glory."

"Really?"

"But of course, dear. That railroad line will be completed, you see. The other one up here is only a pipe dream. The backers haven't enough capital to build through. And without a railroad these camps will fail." She quit brushing and turned to face him, all the lightness gone from her expression now, replaced by a hard-edged, shrewd intelligence. Perhaps, he reflected, poor Aggie couldn't compete with this woman even in that arena. "Have you heard anything different from that, Longarm?"

He shrugged. "Actually what I heard from a local mover and shaker just tonight is that without a railroad these camps will die, all right."

"Exactly," Leah said.

"Oh th' other hand," Longarm said, "this fella wasn't at all convinced that they won't get their railroad built. The only reason there's doubt is because money they were counting on t' finance laying track was stolen. But he says they can recoup those losses if they hang tough. Tell you the truth, Leah, I believed him. He sounded like he knew what he was talking about."

"How odd," she said, "when my sources in Glory told me just the opposite."

"Aw, rivalry between small towns like these is pretty common. Why, I've seen things get s' bad they started shooting at each other. And county seats? Lordy, you wouldn't believe what some folks will do t' get a county seat. Or hold onta one. Town over in Kansas, the people from one town snuck in one night an' raided the courthouse. Carried off records, files, maps, benches, plat books, everything but the building itself. Come t' think of it, they took some parts o' that too. Folks woke up the next morning an' discovered their county seat was twenty miles away. Never got it back neither, not so far as I heard. The ones that stole it forced an election an' managed to keep it once they had it."

"That's crazy," Leah said.

"Sure it is. Which is what I'm telling you. Folks can be crazy sometimes. So don't get caught in the middle of some rivalry between two little towns when each of 'em wants you to think theirs is the only one worth looking at. Could be the both of 'em will do just fine."

"That certainly wasn't the impression I got from the people in Glory. They were quite positive Snowshoe won't get its railroad and that I should avoid investing here."

Longarm shrugged. "Makes no never mind t' me either way," he told her quite honestly. "My business only has t' do with right and wrong, thank goodness. I don't have to care a damn thing about profit or loss."

"Lucky you."

"I do agree, ma'am."

They heard a tapping at the door. Leah was still busy brushing her hair. "Do you want to get it, Longarm?"

"I will if you want me to," he said. "But it'll break the kid's heart if I do."

Leah laughed. "We wouldn't want to be responsible for that, would we?" She set her brush aside, glanced down to make sure that the front of her gown was drawn modestly closed—her previous tough talk on the subject aside—and went to open the door so the bellboy could bring their coffee and champagne in.

The look in the kid's eyes when he saw Leah with her hair just brushed and flowing loose and gleaming made Longarm glad that he hadn't gone to the door. Leah was the kind of woman dreams were built on. And no doubt this youngster had just received a lifetime supply of 'em. No harm in that, Longarm figured.

"Your supper will be up real soon, ma'am," the boy managed in a cracking voice. He looked like he was fixing to swoon dead away. "I won't let nothing get cold, I promise."

"I shall trust you to take care of everything," she said in her sultry, throaty voice. "Everything, yes?"

The boy's face turned red. He spun around and practically bolted out of the room. Longarm and Leah waited until he was gone and well out of hearing before they broke into laughter.

Chapter 34

Leah really didn't mind if the whole world knew about her interest in the tall deputy. Come morning she insisted that they go down to breakfast together and the hell with anything that might be said about it. It was an invitation that Longarm would have declined if he could, but not the sort a gentleman could reasonably refuse. They parted only long enough for him to go to his own room for a quick shave, agreeing to meet in the hotel dining room in twenty minutes.

When Longarm walked into the dining room, Leah was already there. She was not alone. He would have backed away except that she saw him in the doorway and motioned him forward.

"Deputy Marshal Custis Long, this is Mr. Ellis Farmer. Mr. Farmer is—"

"Oh, Mr. Farmer and I have already met," Longarm said with a tight smile that was pure politeness extended for Leah's sake. Longarm hadn't liked the editor of the *Snowshoe Independent* when they'd first met, and he hadn't found any cause to change that opinion since.

"How nice," Leah said.

Farmer's expression showed that he was somewhat less pleased with it than the lady was. Apparently he thought about as much of Longarm as Longarm did of him.

"Sit down, dear, before your coffee gets cold."

Longarm grunted and took a seat directly across the table from Farmer where he could stare some daggers at

the big-mouthed, lying, rabble-rousing sonuvabitch. Farmer
didn't care for that, and quickly began to examine the
weave in the tablecloth under his nose rather than meet
Longarm's eyes.

"I can see that I'm interrupting your breakfast," the
newspaperman said.

"Nonsense," Leah chirped, oblivious to the hackles that
were rising on both sides of her. "I have no need to keep
secrets from Longarm, Mr. Farmer. Please go ahead with
your explanation."

"I . . . really, Miss Skelde, I would prefer to do this some
other time."

Leah shrugged. "If you wish." Her offhanded manner
said Farmer's business wasn't all that important to her.

"I do, thank you." Farmer stood, bowing over Leah's
hand and doing his best to ignore Longarm. "Later this
morning if that would be convenient?"

"Whatever," Leah said with another shrug of dismissal.
Before Farmer had gotten two steps away she was telling
Longarm, "I understand they have fresh roe today, dear.
How would scrambled eggs and fried roe sound?"

Longarm's response was that it sounded quite frankly
like shit. Except out loud he didn't say it exactly that
way. "Doesn't quite do it for me today. But don't you
fret. I'll think of something that sounds good." He picked
up a neatly lettered menu card and began looking it over.
"What's the deal with Farmer if you don't mind me asking?
I thought you'd decided you wouldn't be doing business
here."

"I won't," she said. "Mr. Farmer heard I plan to open
several, um, business establishments in Glory and Silver
Creek. He has an advertising scheme worked out and wants
me to contract with him for it. Discreet newspaper ads,
contract printing for handbills, things like that. I don't
know the details yet, of course. We hadn't gone that far.
He seems to think he can offer me bargain rates in exchange
for a long-term contract commitment. Naturally I need to
see some details before I can even consider his proposals."

She looked up from her menu card and frowned slightly. "Odd how he left like that, isn't it? And he had seemed so anxious to talk to me. Oh, well."

"Why would you think about advertising here or passing circulars out in Snowshoe anyway?"

"Why, I wouldn't. Naturally not. There would be no point in it," Leah said.

"I'm confused."

"Mr. Farmer is going to be operating the newspapers in all the towns served by the Silver Creek, Tipson, and Glory Rail Road. Some sort of monopoly arrangement he worked out with Edgar Monroe."

"Pardon? I mean, who is Edgar Monroe and what does he have t' do with anything?"

"I'm sure you remember Mr. Monroe, Longarm. You got into a fistfight with him in defense of my honor." She winked. "That was back when you still thought I might have some honor, if you recall."

Monroe, then, would be the railroad boss who had ridden from Silver Creek to Glory with them a few days earlier. Yeah, Longarm remembered the man, all right. "You say the newspaperman from here worked out an arrangement with Monroe about running papers down in those other towns too?"

"Not in addition to the Snowshoe newspaper, I shouldn't think," Leah corrected. "After all, both those gentlemen assured me that Snowshoe is on the decline. They expect it to disappear altogether within the year."

"They do?"

"Oh, yes. Didn't I tell you all of this before?"

"Yeah, I guess you did. Farmer, though . . ."

"Is something wrong, Longarm? You look so serious."

He shook his head and tried to force a smile. He suspected it turned out to be a pretty weak one, but he gave it his best shot. "Just thinking. That's all."

Leah shrugged again, obviously not much giving a damn who did business or where it was done just so long as she could manage her own affairs in peace.

161

A waiter came and they ordered breakfast—Longarm was able to resist Leah's suggestion about the fish eggs—and idly chatted about the changes taking place in Denver while they waited for the meal. It turned out that they had several acquaintances in common both there and in Kansas. Leah was a woman of wide travels and great conviviality. She was very careful, though. No one she mentioned by name could possibly have been hurt by the acquaintance. Longarm suspected there were many others who enjoyed the lady's friendship but whose names would remain in confidence with her.

The talk diminished while they ate, then resumed once the plates had been exchanged for final cups of fresh coffee. Longarm leaned back and lighted a cheroot. This wasn't a bad way to start one's day, he figured.

"Miss Leah?"

Longarm turned his head to see a wildly grinning Parson George rush into the dining room.

"Miss Leah, is it really you?"

Leah jumped up and gave Parson a hug as the big, ugly night stalker reached her. She looked to be just as happy as Parson was about this meeting, and from what Longarm could gather from their conversation, they were friends of very long standing.

"Haven't seen you since . . . but did you hear about . . . someone told me that she . . . five years, but he'll be out in two . . . no, but I was told that she . . ."

Longarm smiled and crossed his legs. He leaned back and drank some coffee. Parson and Leah would get around to remembering him eventually.

The explanations came when they did. Parson and Leah went as far back as Leah's first shyly hesitant, frightened forays into "the life," as they called it. It was the woman called Sally who'd "turned out" Leah. Parson had been working for Sally even then. He had befriended the beautiful but scared young girl, and was her protector as well as her friend for as long as Leah remained with Sally. Now Leah was especially

162

pleased to discover that Parson and Longarm were already friends too.

"But, darling, I can't wait to see her again. You will take me, won't you, dear? At once?"

"Quick as I do what she sent me here for," Parson agreed.

"Then hurry up with it, whatever it is. I can't wait to see Sal again, darling. You will excuse us, won't you, Longarm?"

"Of course I will, Leah. I got work t' do."

"More of it than you might think today, Longarm," Parson put in. "That's what Miz Sally sent me here about. T' find you, Longarm."

"Oh?"

He grinned. "One of the boys guarding your Indians couldn't stand it no more. He got horny and snuck into town last night. Miz Sally says I should tell you that the Indians are being held at the old Crane mine. Wherever that is. She had some miner fella draw up a map for you." Parson produced a crudely sketched map and gave it to Longarm. "Is there anything else you need from me, Longarm?"

"Just to see you and Leah enjoy this chance meeting. And thanks, Parson. Please tell the lady that I appreciate all she's done to help."

"I'll do that, Longarm." He said it over his shoulder. He and Leah were already on their way out.

Longarm stubbed his cheroot out in an empty butter dish and reached for his hat. Now that he knew where the Utes were he could get this business finished.

"Sir?" a voice called from behind him before he had gotten three steps in the direction of the door.

"The bill for the breakfasts, sir?"

Longarm chuckled. A little while ago Leah had made a big point of saying how well she was doing and that he was to eat hearty because this was gonna be her treat. Steak, caviar, roe, champagne cocktails with breakfast, anything he wanted. It seemed the distraction of seeing Parson and

163

finding out that Sally was in town had taken that right out of mind. Not that he was complaining.

"Put it on my hotel bill," Longarm told the waiter. Hell, let the government pay for it. The cost was worth it if it helped him find those Utes. Making that claim was only stretching things a little way. "And add something for yourself too."

"Thank you, sir."

Longarm's stride lengthened once he reached the door. He was debating with himself over whether he should tell Lawyer Able about this or wait so he could go to the mine alone and not have to argue about that. He didn't want to drag Aggie into a gun fight. Better, he decided, to wait. He turned toward the livery stable instead of heading for the house where Aggie was staying.

Chapter 35

As armed camps go, this one was kinda pathetic.

Longarm sat on the hillside behind a scrub oak and smoked a cheroot while he looked the situation over.

There were supposed to be four guards at the mine. He could see two. One of those had taken a chair and folding table over to the gate and was playing a card game with an Indian. The other guard looked more asleep than not, although he did have a carbine laid across his lap. That obviously qualified him as a guard.

The way the Utes were acting inside the makeshift palisade around the mine opening, they might've been willing to take guard shifts themselves. The flimsy structure could have been pushed down by any self-respecting six-year-old, and while Longarm watched, two young women came out through the gate—unchallenged, and in fact barely noticed by the guards—and helped themselves to fresh water from the stream below the Crane mine.

This was . . . Longarm scratched his ear and frowned . . . he wasn't sure what this was. But what it *wasn't* was anything close to what he might've expected to see here.

After everything he'd been told in town about the people hating and fearing the Ute tribe, well, this scene just wasn't natural.

Aggie had actually been worried about mobs of townspeople slaughtering the Indians if the writ were served? Boring them to death seemed more likely from what Longarm could see here.

There was only one way to get any explanations. Longarm

stood and walked down in plain sight of the people below.

It was the Indian cardplayer who noticed his approach and pointed it out to the guard, who seemed to be his enemy only when it came to gin rummy.

"Aw, hell. Are you the deputy marshal from Denver?" the guard asked.

"Uh, huh."

"Bud, Reece, Anthony? Dammit, Bud, wake up there. And you boys come outta the shack now. The deputy is here."

"Who are you?" Longarm asked.

The man grinned and extended his hand. "Brad Crannock, Deputy. I'm Chief Bevvy's second in command. Nice to meet you."

"Brad, I swear I'm getting more confused all the time. I was expecting to be met with bullets here and have to fight my way in to free the Utes. Now you're acting like we all been playing some kinda damn game."

"Not a game, Deputy. But not so serious as we'd been told neither. I mean, hell, once we got acquainted with Wind's people it turned out that, shit, they wasn't wanting to scalp nobody."

"Wind?" Longarm asked.

"Sure. The headman of the Utes here, Man Who Breaks Wind."

Longarm chuckled. Breaks Wind. That must be Aggie's Bray Swind, misunderstood when one of the Utes had been trying to speak English. Longarm kinda liked the real name better than Aggie's term anyhow. "Go ahead," he said. "Sorry I interrupted you."

"Okay," Crannock said, picking up where he'd left off. "By the time we got comfortable enough around the Utes to figure that out, all this court stuff was already going on. And then we learned that you federal boys didn't want it stopped and—"

"Whoa!" Longarm barked. "Now you stop right there." He glanced around. The other guards had come over to join them now, and they were surrounded by placid, well-fed

Ute Indians as well. "What was it you just said, mister?"

"About what?"

"About the federal government wanting this shit t' continue, that's what."

"Well, of course I said that. I mean, it's true. Right?"

"Wrong."

Crannock frowned. "But we were told real plain, Deputy, that the U.S. government wanted this to play all the way. So there'd be a, uh, precedent, they call it. That's when all the courts have to rule some particular way because some other court has already—"

"I know what a precedent is," Longarm injected.

"Okay. Well, that's what we're working out here is, a precedent. Hell, it was your idea, not ours. Once we saw how things really were, well, we didn't want to keep Wind and his folks no more. But we was told you didn't want 'em turned loose for a while yet. Not till there was time for that Nebraska writ to be tested on appeal. And that you were only gonna go through the motions of serving the thing until then, so we should pretend to not cooperate with you. We all agreed to go along with it. Wind an' his people been camping out here, more or less, and we been setting around looking like guards in case somebody official came by and—"

"The Indians' own lawyer let you get away with something like that?" Longarm blurted out. He found it a little hard to accept that Aggie could have been playacting her part of the deception all this time.

"Oh, we couldn't let Miz Able find out. She's a prissy kinda bitch and not always very understanding about things. She wouldn't have gone along with it at all. Anyway, I got to say that it couldn't of come at a better time far as we're concerned. We got all we can pray over trying to solve the train robbery, you know, and—"

"Forget the train robbery," Longarm said. "Who the hell told you a stupid think like that about the court precedents and appeals and shit?"

Brad Crannock gave Longarm a puzzled look. Then he commenced to talking.

Chapter 36

"Are you sure?"

"Dammit, Boo, you oughta know better than to ask that question of a lawman. Ain't no peace officer ever been sure of anything. Nor allowed t' be," Longarm said. "It's only courts that have the privilege of being sure. But I'm sure enough that I'm willing to make the arrests and let a court sort out the right from the wrong of it."

"I'm not so sure about the jurisdiction, Long. After all—"

"That part I am sure of. Don't you worry 'bout that. I can claim all kinds of jurisdiction here. Might have to lay some strange charges down, but there's reason enough. It will stick."

"If you say so." The Snowshoe chief of police didn't sound particularly happy, though, in spite of the mission Longarm had enlisted him and his people to take a hand in.

But then very few people enjoy being subjected to day-long hikes in the mountains.

Longarm stepped the pace up and moved along at a steady clip, leaving a string of disgruntled Snowshoe men behind, all of them deputized twice over, first on behalf of the town and now under federal authority.

Of course Longarm was sure, though.

He'd been confused as hell to begin with. But no longer. Not since he'd had a chance to talk with old Man Who Breaks Wind.

The Ute headman hadn't had but a few words of English— the usual assortment of whoa, haw, gee, hello, fuck you—but

168

there was a young warrior-to-be who used to attend Sunday school with the Meeker family who had a fair grasp of the language. He was a bright kid, smiling and agreeable. He was quick to point out that he hadn't killed anyone during the recent unpleasantness at the agency. After all, killing was wrong. He'd learned that in Sunday school. On the other hand, one of the things he was most proud of was that he personally had raped more white women than any other Ute he knew of. It was a distinction that he believed conveyed a certain amount of honor and dignity. Longarm had had to remind himself that that was water over the dam. Military and civil authority alike had exacted all the punishments that would ever be required.

Fortunately, Longarm's interests lay in what the old headman could tell him and not in the things the youngster wanted to brag about.

The Utes were more than willing to leave the vicinity of Snowshoe now, and thus alleviate any of the fears that had been stirred up by Ellis Farmer in his newspaper or by anyone else by way of whisperings and innuendo.

After all, the band had been on their way out of the mountains when they'd seen those peculiar white men and first gotten into trouble.

Longarm's interest had definitely quickened when Man Who Breaks Wind brought up the band's confrontation with a group of whites.

Because by then Longarm believed he knew what was coming. But he waited for Man Who Breaks Wind to confirm what Longarm already suspected.

A few matter-of-fact sentences offered by Man Who Breaks Wind. A few routine questions by Longarm. Then the tall deputy had stood and reached for cheroots to share among the Utes.

"You are free to go in peace, Grandfather," he told Man Who Breaks Wind. "May your spring hunt be a good one. May all your wives be fertile. You have been much help to the Great Father in Washington."

"Big help?"

169

"Big help."

Man Who Breaks Wind grinned and said something to the people who had gathered close behind to listen in on the conversation between their own leader and the trusted white man they knew as Long Arm.

Longarm had gone through the motions of formally presenting Brad Crannock with the writ of habeas corpus that granted the Utes their freedom.

Then he'd said, "Now, Brad, you'd best take me to Chief Bevvy about as quick as you can. If you think he'd like to clear that train robbery off his books and maybe make some recovery of the stolen gold, that is."

"If I think he'd . . . shit, I reckon. Grab your guns and let's go, boys," Crannock had said.

Now, half a day later, Crannock's men, Boo Bevvy and his posse, and Longarm were all footsore and sweating, but were still marching along at a steady rate.

With any kind of luck, Longarm figured, they should have everything over and done with before the witching hour tonight.

With or without bloodshed. Longarm frankly didn't much give a damn which.

Chapter 37

"I'm going to report you to your superiors. I want you to know that," the conductor hissed.

Longarm plucked a pencil stub out of the conductor's pocket, borrowed a scrap of paper from Boo Bevvy, and wrote down Billy Vail's name and office address. He handed it to the train conductor. "If you want to go any higher than that try the Attorney General. I don't know the address offhand, but I reckon you can look it up. Someplace in the District o' Columbia."

"Don't think I won't report you," the conductor threatened again. "You've commandeered this train under protest, sir. Under protest."

"Mister, before your letter ever has time t' get there, I'll already have reported the whole thing myself. Count on it." Longarm winked at Police Chief Bevvy and looked back through the narrow passenger coach. All the men seemed awake. But then they would be. They all knew they were riding toward a good likelihood of gunsmoke and hot lead. A man tends to pay attention when that's what he expects to see in front of him soon.

"How far?" Longarm asked the conductor.

"I won't tell you."

"All right." Longarm leaned out of the window and tried to look ahead down the tracks, but the night was dark and all he could see up front was a yellow glow coming from the engineer's cab and a pale white glow farther ahead from the weak carbide lamp mounted on the front of the small engine.

171

"You want me to arrest him, Longarm?" Bevvy suggested.

"What charge?"

"Obstructing justice."

"It wouldn't hold up in court."

"No, but it might be three, four weeks before the judge has time to hear the case. He'd have to sit in jail until then."

"You do what you think best, Boo."

"Four miles," the conductor said quickly. "Uh, more or less."

"Thank you."

The conductor turned and beat a retreat in the direction of the tiny caboose. Bevvy winked at Longarm and got a grin back.

"We'll be in Tipson in ten minutes or less," Bevvy called to the men in the coach. "Everybody get ready."

There was a rattle of steel clashing on steel when Winchester levers were cranked as the posse members checked the function of their guns. Others snapped shotgun breeches open to inspect their chambers and make sure the guns were charged with man-sized buckshot and not puny bird shot. If there was any shooting tonight it would be to kill, not to scare.

"Five minutes," Bevvy called out.

"Remember, dammit, don't any of you start anything," Longarm reminded them. "I'm taking responsibility for this, so don't none of you jump the gun on me. We'll do this nice and easy if we can, or the hard way only if we have to."

A few of the possemen looked like they would have preferred to go it the hard way regardless, but those men were in the minority.

Bevvy leaned out and peered ahead. "I can see the town lights. Less than a mile to go. Everybody get ready now."

Somewhere ahead the engineer—under close guard and thorough instruction—closed his throttle and passed a signal for the brakemen to tighten their wheels. The entire inventory of rolling stock belonging to the Silver Creek, Tipson, and Glory Narrow Gauge Rail Road began to slow for its arrival in Tipson.

Chapter 38

All they had to do to find the smelter was to follow
their noses. Literally. The place stank of sulfuric acid
and wood smoke. Wood, not coal. The difference was
important, Longarm knew. Trying to operate a smelter
without coal—which couldn't be hauled in until or unless
the railroad was put through; wood was a resource that was
quickly exhausted in the vicinity of any mining town—was a
makeshift proposition. A desperation gamble that the people
there believed would pay off, now that they had their own
ore concentrates to process, plus whatever they could steal
from Snowshoe and the other high-mountain towns.

"Quiet now. Let's do this easy if we can," Longarm
cautioned.

He guided the posse—at this point it was his posse, not
Police Chief Bevvy's, and had to remain so for purposes of
jurisdiction since Bevvy had no authority there and would
not have until Longarm's suspicions were confirmed—into
position surrounding the Tipson smelter.

Despite the late hour the smelter was operating at full
speed. Smoke poured from its chimneys. The inside of the
big, barnlike structure was alive with light and noise and
noxious fumes. Longarm's nose wrinkled as he approached
the door. "I'll go in first, Boo. You cover me and give the
signal for the rest of them to rush in if anything happens."

Bevvy nodded.

Longarm stood outside for one moment longer. He held
his badge displayed in the palm of his left hand where

anyone could see. His right hand held his Colt revolver. "Ready."

"Go," Bevvy said.

Longarm kicked the door open and stepped through.

"Freeze! United States marshals here. No one gets hurt unless you start it."

The two guards who were supposed to prevent un- authorized entry were caught flat-footed. So were the workmen who were within sight or hearing of the door.

"Stand easy. We'll work out in a minute who's under arrest here and who isn't." Longarm sidled out of the doorway and motioned with his left hand. Boo Bevvy and half a dozen Snowshoe possemen poured in with shotguns held at the ready. It probably helped that each of them was already wearing a badge issued by the town of Snowshoe. It wouldn't matter that that wasn't who Longarm had said they all were. The startled smelter workers wouldn't be thinking of such details. Not yet. All they would be seeing would be gun muzzles and steely eyes, never mind the rest of it.

"That's fine, boys. All of you with guns, pile them on that table there. That's right, thank you. Yes, you too, dammit. Thank you."

The smelter men managed to divest themselves of their weapons in practically no time at all. Perfect. Longarm would be pleased if he could bring this whole thing off with not a shot being fired.

By the time all the employees had been rounded up and all the firearms collected, the smelter files had been located and the cabinets jimmied open.

"Well?" Longarm asked.

"It's probably here," one of the possemen said. He had been selected for this chore because his everyday job was as comptroller of Ames Delacoutt's mine in Snowshoe. He was a man who knew his way around ledger entries the way Longarm knew his way around good horses or bad men. "But it's going to take some long, serious study to nail it all down, Marshal. I have to cross-reference all the inventory and production records and sort out all the receipted concentrates. I can do it, of course. They couldn't possibly hide all those tons of concentrates they took from us. The work will be reflected somewhere in these records, I promise you."

Longarm looked at the silent, fuming men of Tipson who were standing now under guard in their own smelter.

It was almighty interesting, he thought, how not a single one of them had bothered to ask what this raid was about.

But then they all knew, didn't they?

And they all accepted as fact that Longarm and the Snowshoe men knew as well.

The way Longarm read it, this failure to protest and question was as damning as any evidence the comptroller from Snowshoe might expose in those records. Although, of course, that form of confirmation would be necessary too once the mess came before a judge and jury.

"Where are the bosses?" Longarm asked.

"Which ones?"

"Let's start with Edgar Monroe."

"He's . . . not here."

"I guessed that much. So where is he?"

"Search me."

"Boo, you heard the man. Have some of your boys take him outside and search him."

"Hey!" the fellow yelped.

"Just remember where we can find Mr. Monroe, did you?"

"I think, uh, I think maybe I did."

Longarm smiled and stepped forward.

Chapter 39

Once again Longarm had Boo Bevvy and a posse of men from Snowshoe at his back. The difference was that this time there were fewer of them. Most of the posse members had been left at the smelter keeping the workmen under guard while the comptroller examined dry, dusty business ledgers line by line. Now only the Snowshoe police chief and four of his best officers were backing the federal man.

"Ready?"

"Go."

Longarm's boot smashed into the door. The lock shattered, and the door was flung back on its hinges.

Longarm was inside, gun in one hand and badge in the other, before the door had time to rebound.

"Nobody move. Federal marshals."

As a collection of conspirators these fellows were a disappointment. They looked like any other bunch of small-time businessmen.

Except maybe a little more nervous than most.

There were five of them at the table. The only one Longarm recognized was Ellis Farmer. Farmer blanched even paler than usual when he saw who had burst in. The other men at the table seemed mostly interested in gaping at the gun muzzles. Farmer kept staring with a certain degree of horror at Chief Bevvy and the other individuals who had been his neighbors in Snowshoe. And whom he had betrayed on behalf of these other men.

"This is an outrage. This is—"

"Shut the fuck up, Andrew." Longarm might not know all the men at the table, but Chief Bevvy knew this one at least.

"You have no right to barge in here like this," another squawked.

"Bullshit," Longarm said. "Lawman has every right to make an arrest."

"We haven't done anything."

"No? Then you won't care that we've impounded the records from that smelter you set up."

"Jesus!" someone blurted out.

"Keep trying, mister. Maybe He'll help you."

"We haven't done anything. Really, Boo. We haven't."

"Cut the crap, Jasper. Deputy Long figured it out. Me and my boys have been going crazy looking for your tracks from where you got away with our gold. Hell, the tracks were in plain sight all the time. Railroad tracks."

"The stupid thing," Longarm put in, "was that those Indians didn't give a damn what a bunch of white men wanted to do. If you'd just left them alone they would have gone on down to the low country and set about their spring hunt. It made no particular impression on them at all when they saw you stealing that gold. They figured you were just so many crazy white men, and hardly any Indian will bother himself trying to figure white men out. If you'd just left them alone another few weeks they would have headed on down for the spring hunt. They sure as hell didn't care enough about what they'd seen the day of the train robbery to tell anyone about it. But no, you got nervous and tried to keep them quiet by hiding them away in legal custody. And you would have started riots or generated any kind of slaughter to accomplish that, spreading those lies about Ute war parties and everything. You dumb bastards. You could've actually started another Indian war with those lies."

"You're responsible for that, Farmer," Bevvy said. "Your neighbors will hold you accountable too. Don't you think otherwise."

177

Farmer had begun to sweat.

Longarm shook his head, disgusted with the whole crowd of them. What the Utes had seen, the reason these men had panicked and orchestrated the series of lies, was the robbers carrying their impossibly bulky loot away from the Bitterroot and Brightwater train. Not by wagon or mule train, but by simple gravity. The train was held up and taken to the point where it most closely approached the right of way of the Silver Creek, Tipson, and Glory hundreds of feet lower in the canyon bottoms. Then the robbers simply slid the boxed concentrates down to be loaded onto the SCT&G cars below. It was that bare slide that Longarm and Leah Skelde had seen when they were waiting for the train to pick them up the other day. From below the marks left behind by the boxes were obvious. But from up above, at the level of the Bitterroot and Brightwater roadbed, there was nothing remarkable that could be seen. The robbers opened the throttle of the stolen train once the boxes were unloaded, and the train was sent down the tracks on its own to stop wherever it ran out of steam. That was where Bevvy and his men found it, and where they assumed the gold concentrates had been unloaded. They hadn't thought to backtrack in search of anything so ordinary as the SCT&G tracks that they saw every time they traveled the B&B right of way. Longarm had been able to put it together only because of that delay between when the coach from Silver Creek dropped passengers off at the end of the tracks and the train from Glory arrived to carry them the rest of the way. Otherwise he never would have seen those drag marks.

Those tipped him to the truth, along with discovering that the man in Snowshoe who was primarily responsible for the Ute scare was the same newspaper editor who suddenly had a vested financial interest in the survival of the SCT&G. Ellis Farmer went out of his way to stir up hard feelings against the Ute tribe. And it had occurred to Longarm too that despite all the violence he'd been told to expect from the townspeople of Snowshoe, the only real trouble

178

he'd experienced came at the hands of outsiders, not from locals at all.

Longarm was sure he could find a whole passel of charges to lodge against each and every one of these conspirators. Molesting Ute Indians—who were, after all, wards of the government and therefore clearly under federal jurisdiction for their protection—would come at the top of that list.

And Bevvy would find plenty more charges to drop on them at the local level. Train robbery would only be for openers.

There was, though, at least one man missing from the group at the table here. One chair sat empty with a stack of papers in front of it and a fat cigar left lying in an ashtray there to drift smoke into the stuffy air inside the room.

"Where's Monroe?" Longarm asked.

"Who?"

"Never mind. Boo, you and your people take care of these prisoners. I'll go find Monroe."

"You think he ran out?"

Longarm grinned. "What I'd bet is that he went out back to take a piss. Bad timing is the only reason we didn't pull him in with the rest of 'em."

"I can come with you."

"No, you and your boys get the cuffs on this bunch. I'll bring Monroe in. And enjoy it, to tell you the truth. Only met the man one time, but even then I felt like I'd disliked him for years."

"We'll see you at the jail," Bevvy said.

Longarm took the hallway toward the back of the saloon building in which the good old boys of Tipson had been meeting, then went downstairs. It was the logical direction anyone looking for an outhouse would take.

A path led from the back door to a one-holer. The saloon management had thoughtfully provided a lantern set on a post halfway between the building and the shitter so patrons wouldn't have to stumble or feel their way along.

Longarm checked the door of the outhouse. It was latched.

"Keep your britches buttoned, damn it. I'm almost done."

Longarm smiled. He recognized the voice. It was the hotshot railroad boss Edgar Monroe, all right. Hotshot in his own opinion anyhow. Longarm happened to think somewhat less of him than that.

"Take your time." Longarm stepped back and waited.

The wait seemed like a very long time, although it probably was no more than a few minutes. After a bit he heard a deep sigh and the creaking of boards as Monroe's weight shifted on the seat. "Ah."

There was another wait, shorter this time, and the sound of the bolt being drawn.

"Next."

Monroe stepped out of the outhouse. And found himself facing Longarm.

"Surprise."

"You!"

"It's my pleasure an' my duty, mister, to place you under arrest."

"No."

"Wrong."

"You can't."

"Sure I can."

"I won't let you."

"Sure you will. Now turn around like a good fella an' put your hands behind you."

"I'm not going to be dragged off like some common criminal."

"You'll get used to it."

"We can talk about this. I'm rich, you know."

"Congratulations. Your wrists, please?"

For a moment Monroe looked like he was going to throw a haymaker. But only for a moment. Perhaps he remembered that the last time he fought this tall deputy he'd lost the contest. Whatever the reason, he held himself stiff and ready for only that moment, and then subsided.

"At least let me have a cigar first. We can . . . talk . . . while I smoke it." Monroe reached inside his coat.

180

Longarm opened his mouth to speak, to tell the idiot to keep his hands out where they could be seen.

Too late.

Monroe's hand flashed with sudden speed, and a nickel-plated revolver appeared in his fist with a magician's speed.

The big man looked smug now. Superior. Lording it over the mere mortal who had dared to oppose Edgar Monroe's wishes. As if he couldn't believe that anyone would have had the temerity to even think he might oppose anyone as rich and as important as Edgar Monroe.

Hell, Longarm couldn't much believe it either. That anybody would be dumb enough to stand there and try to take him in a face-to-face draw like that. Stupid.

The big Colt bellowed before Monroe's little rimfire had time to speak.

The two men were standing at devastatingly close range. At that distance the .44 slug had an impact that must have felt like Monroe stepped in front of one of his own trains.

The bullet riding the tip of a lance of yellow fire slammed into Monroe's chest with crushing force.

It knocked him backward and spun him halfway around so that he was facing the other direction now. His momentum carried him on toward the outhouse he had just left. One tottering step and then another.

He pitched forward and down. Face first.

"Aw, shit," Longarm said aloud as Monroe tumbled back inside the outhouse.

The heavy body crashed down onto a much too flimsy seat. Wood splintered and broke with a loud crack, and Monroe fell with his torso hanging over the deep toilet sink.

Hanging there only for an instant. Then sliding forward. And down.

Longarm made a face.

There was a splash, and a truly vile stench flowed from the outhouse in an almost visible wave. Longarm didn't think he'd ever smelled anything quite that bad before. And if he had, he damn sure didn't want to remember it now.

The only things he could see of Edgar Monroe's body now were the man's shiny, polished shoes and his stocking-clad ankles.

"I sure as hell hope you was dead before you went in there," Longarm told the corpse in a soft voice. "Because I sure as hell ain't gonna treat you like no drowning victim an' try to revive you."

He turned and went in search of the local jail. He was to meet Bevvy there. Quick as they could get things wrapped up, Longarm figured they could start back to Snowshoe. He had some things to tell Aggie Able about her clients—who by now should be miles along on their annual journey down to their spring hunting grounds—and there were certain other things he would like to discuss with Leah. But those things would be private and had nothing to do with Indians or robbers or would-be assassins. And the way Longarm saw it, they would be *much* more interesting than anything he and Aggie might talk about.

Watch for

LONGARM AND THE GRAVE ROBBERS

155th in the bold LONGARM series from Jove

Coming in November!

WESTERNS!

at least a savings of $3.00 each month below the publishers price. Second, there is never any shipping, handling or other hidden charges—Free home delivery. What's more there is no minimum number of books you must buy, you may return any selection for full credit and you can cancel your subscription at any time. A TRUE VALUE!

Mail the coupon below

To start your subscription and receive 2 FREE WESTERNS, fill out the coupon below and mail it today. We'll send your first shipment which includes 2 FREE BOOKS as soon as we receive it.

Mail To:
True Value Home Subscription Services, Inc.   **10689**
P.O. Box 5235
120 Brighton Road
Clifton, New Jersey 07015-5235

YES! I want to start receiving the very best Westerns being published today. Send me my first shipment of 6 Westerns for me to preview FREE for 10 days. If I decide to keep them, I'll pay for just 4 of the books at the low subscriber price of $2.45 each; a total of $9.80 (a $17.70 value). Then each month I'll receive the 6 newest and best Westerns to preview Free for 10 days. If I'm not satisfied I may return them within 10 days and owe nothing. Otherwise I'll be billed at the special low subscriber rate of $2.45 each; a total of $14.70 (at least a $17.70 value) and save $3.00 off the publishers price. There are never any shipping, handling or other hidden charges. I understand I am under no obligation to purchase any number of books and I can cancel my subscription at any time, no questions asked. In any case the 2 FREE books are mine to keep.

Name _____

Address _____ Apt. # _____

City _____ State _____ Zip _____

Telephone # _____

Signature _____
(if under 18 parent or guardian must sign)
Terms and prices subject to change.
Orders subject to acceptance by True Value Home Subscription Services, Inc.